audrey

THE STEEL SISTERS

THE DAUGHTER'S OF JUDGE STEEL

KELLY MOORE

EDITED BY
KERRY GENOVA

ILLUSTRATED BY
DARK WATER COVERS

Kelly Moore

title

Audrey

THE *Steel* SISTERS

BESTSELLING AUTHOR
KELLY MOORE

playlist

The Joker by the Steve Miller Band

    Love The Hell Out of You by Lewis Capaldi

    Shallow by Lewis Capaldi

    If I Would Have Known by Kyle Hume

    Not Used to Normal by Jillian Rossi

    Spirit Lead Me Where My Trust Is Without Borders by Raspo

    The Scientist by Raspo

    Hush Little Baby Don't You Cry by Young Joe

    Only Light by Vanacore Music

family
introduction

Meet the Steel clan. Sisters Finley, James, Audrey, and their enigmatic father, Judge Benjamin Steel. To outsiders, they are an average family. But this family leads a secret double life.

By day, they navigate professional jobs with corporate elites and attend lavish galas. By night, they transform into modern-day Robin Hoods, executing daring heists to reclaim ill-gotten gains and redistributing them to the deserving.

Their story blurs the lines between crime and justice in a thrilling tale of modern-day renegades. The burning question is: can they sustain their high-stakes exploits without getting ensnared in a web of their own making?

Join the Steel family in this heart-pounding, morally complex adventure where the line between right and wrong becomes a thrilling gray area.

Prologue

THE ROOM IS DIMLY LIT because the light hurts her dry, green eyes, and her skin feels like a frigid day at the beginning of winter. Lips so blue they are almost purple. My gut claws at itself from within, gnarled with emotions I've kept locked inside me to keep a brave face on for my three daughters, who are curled up next to their dying mother in her hospital bed, not fully understanding what they will be losing today. I'd trade places with her frail body in a heartbeat. My life for hers seems like a reasonable trade.

Her cancer, like a beast, slithered its way into her body with powerful fingers, growing as if it were watered with fertilizer daily. I see it as an entity that exists only to destroy our lives, and it takes without apology, without pity, and definitely no mercy. It's like her body breathed life into the cancer cells, bursting through every tissue, falling in love with her.

My lips tremble, and I rub them together, thinking about the rest of our lives without her in it. She keeps telling me that God is calling her home, and I'm pretty damn pissed off about it. It's not fair. She's the good one, not me. I'm a worthless man without my sweet wife. How do you say goodbye to the person who shares your soul? Heartbreak doesn't begin to describe what I'm feeling. More like profound desolation with immeasurable misery.

Her breathing is shallow and more labored than it was an hour ago, and with each passing beat of her heart, she's slipping away, and I'm completely helpless to save her.

Bits and pieces of our lives surge through my mind, trying to recall every single moment, not wanting to forget. Like the day I married the most beautiful soul I'd ever met. Why she ever fell in love with the likes of me, I'll never understand. She was pure goodness, and I was a man teetering on a fine line between good and downright evil. She drew out the moral man inside me, knocking the devil off my shoulder.

She filled our lives with three beautiful girls. I swallow the sharp coolness in my throat and laugh to myself about how badly I wanted sons. So much so that I gave our first two daughters boys' names because we never agreed on any others. By the time the third popped out, I had resigned myself to the fact that I was a girl dad and named Audrey after my dear, sweet grandmother. My wife secretly believes she's my favorite of the three. She reminds me more of Violet than the other two. Even at two years old, I can see her passion and determination in her personality, yet at the same time, she's sweet and tenderhearted, having her mother's beauty.

"What's that noise, Daddy?" James peers up at me with pools of tears swimming in her bloodshot, puffy eyes.

I blink repeatedly and clear a sob from my throat. "It's Mommy's monitor, telling her she needs to take a breath." I lean over, pressing my forehead to Violet's. "Breathe, baby. Don't give up. We all need you. I don't know how to raise them by myself," I murmur with a whimper next to her ear, knowing what I'm begging of her is impossible, yet I can't stop my desperate plea for her to keep fighting the war inside her body. I rest my forehead against her cool one.

Her eyes flutter open, remaining half hooded, and her mouth slowly forms a smile at the corners. "I love you all so much," she rasps, licking her lips. "It's time," she barely whispers. "Time to let me go."

She's the brave one, not me, and it guts me.

Finley, our oldest, sobs uncontrollably, soaking her mother's gown. Violet weakly bends her arm and lays her hand in Finley's unruly curly hair. "Remember what I told you, sweet girl. Whenever you miss me, I'll be in your heart."

Finley clings to the heart-shaped locket dangling from her necklace and holds it tightly in her hand. Violet had her heartbeat recorded, and you can feel it within the heart-shaped locket. She made one for each of the girls so they'd feel close to her when she's gone. I remember when she showed them to me. I broke down crying at her feet, begging her not to leave us.

James and Finley will remember her, but it breaks my heart that Audrey will only have pictures to remind her of what she lost, and she'll never know how wonderful her mother was to her.

I stand tall, clutching my fists at my side, my pulse picking up its pace when light shines in the room and the doctor eases inside. He has no right to be here after the shit care he's given her.

"Girls, I need you to go out into the hallway so that I can speak to the doctor." Anguish pours out in my tone.

"I don't want to leave Mommy," James cries.

"It's only for a moment, baby."

Finley props Audrey on her hip, captures James's hand in hers, and walks them out of the room.

As soon as the door closes, I get in his face. "You're seriously going to let my wife die because of money?" My croaky voice is laced with bitterness, and spittle builds up in the corners of my mouth. It's everything I can do to refrain myself from squeezing the life out of him.

"I'm sorry, Mr. Steel, but my hands are tied. You don't have insurance, and the treatments that could save her life require a substantial amount of money."

"I told you I can get a loan. I just needed more time!" My guttural roar fills the gap between us while I move protectively to Violet's bedside and weave my hand into hers.

"Unfortunately, you weren't able to meet the deadline, and your wife took an unexpected turn for the worse, not leaving you any more time."

"This is her life we're talking about! It's worth far more than money!" My lip curls into a sneer, unable to control the tears streaming down my face. "Her blood is on your hands!"

"I don't make the rules, Mr. Steel."

"Then who does!" I yell, and Violet squeezes my hand.

"It's too late," she whispers.

"But you know the treatments would have saved her life." My tone changes to pleading for mercy from this man who swore an oath to do no harm.

"Yes," he finally says, locking his gaze on the floor so he doesn't have to look me in the face.

"I'd give you my life and all the money in the world if I possessed it." My legs weaken from pure agony, and I fall to my knees, pressing my hands together as if I'm praying. "Please help her, I besiege you."

"I'm so sorry, Mr. Steel. There isn't anything that can be done at this point to treat Violet."

"You're sorry? My wife is dying, and you've stood by for months watching her deteriorate and did nothing about it!"

"All I can do now is keep her comfortable."

I leap to my feet and grab him by the collar, pushing him against the wall. "You don't deserve to call yourself a doctor for putting the almighty dollar over my wife's life." My nostrils flare, and my lips pull back, baring my teeth. I fight everything inside me not to punch him in the face.

I let go of his white jacket when another alarm buzzes and bolt to my wife's side. "I'm here, baby."

The doctor exits the room with lightning speed, and the girls run inside, climbing back into their mother's bed.

Violet licks her parched lips and her hand trembles in mine. "I will always love you and our girls."

"And we will always love you, baby," I sniff, wiping my tears with my shoulder, then brush her hair off her forehead.

Shakily, she lifts her hand to my chin. "I will leave this world only having one regret. That I wasn't here long enough. The day I married you was the best decision I ever made. You've loved me unconditionally, and our girls are so lucky to have you. I know you're angry at the world right now, but please don't let it change the man I love." She's so weak her hand falls loosely back to the bed. "I love you, Benny. Our girls love you. Don't let your heart stay bitter too long. They need you."

"I hate what they've done to you all for the sake of money. I'm sorry I wasn't a better provider." I ease next to her with Audrey's head in my lap.

"You've given me everything I've ever wanted

and more. I've had a beautiful life with you and our girls."

"I promise I'll take good care of them. I'll find a way for our daughters to have a better life than living in our run-down trailer."

"I love our home." She closes her eyes, and I watch her heart rate slow down on the monitor until it no longer exists. My heart seizes, and I struggle to draw air into my lungs.

"Momma, please don't go," Finley cries, holding on to her for dear life.

James doesn't utter a word through her sobs.

Her final breath peacefully leaves her body, and I feel like it takes mine with her. I gather my girls in my arms. The four of us cling to her and cry. A brief numbness hits me, trying to comfort our girls.

Violet was my lifeline and made me a better man. Numbness flees, and hell-fire fury takes its place, lodging itself in my chest, breathing a life all its own.

"I'm going to give you girls a moment alone with your mother. There's something I have to do. Stay here, and don't leave this room."

I burst into the hallway, my steps echoing loudly on the tiled floor. I rush forward, not halting until I've reached the doctor, gripping his arm tightly and forcefully pulling him in my direction. "My wife is gone, you heartless bastard, and she was the only thread holding my sanity together! You and every person involved in her care will answer for her death, even if it takes the entirety of my life!" I release him but punctuate my words with a pointed finger to his chest. "I want you to never forget the name Benjamin Steel, for I will return to haunt you!"

In that solitary moment, my fate etches itself deep within me, leaving an indelible mark of relentless retribution on my soul.

.

Chapter 1
AUDREY

Current year

THE GAS PEDAL of my bright yellow Bugatti Veyron is too easily manipulated to the floorboard for my own good. North Ocean Drive weaves along the coast, and it's the quickest way to my house. Blue lights swirl when I cross over the bridge, going seventy miles an hour.

"Shit!" I shift into gear, not to slow down, but to lose him, fearing the wrath of my father far worse than the police. Besides, this is a lot more fun. A ticket would be nothing to me, but the chase is intoxicating to my addictive personality and need for adventure.

I turn into an upscale neighborhood, squealing my tires and slowing long enough for the cop to make the same turn at a much slower speed. Making a hard left, the engine races down the narrow road and then another left, exiting the residential area. Leaving the blue lights in the distance, I back onto North Ocean Drive. Taking an immediate left on our long, private, gated driveway, I ease off the pedal and peer through my rearview mirror to see the police car fly by our entrance. I wait to make sure he doesn't turn around before I continue down the drive line with tall palm trees to a circular drive and park in the garage, pushing the button on the visor and closing the glass panel door behind me.

"You did great, girl." I kiss the tips of my fingers and tap the steering wheel. "You are worth the three million I spent to make you mine." Tossing my leather bag over my shoulder, I run up the three steps to enter the house, knowing I'm late.

"It's about damn time you showed up, Audrey." My father taps his watch like he does when he's irritated with my tardiness at our family meetings. And to boot, he called me by my name rather than Audey. It's his telltale sign I've pushed his patience.

"I'm here now, Judge. That's all that matters." I brush my hands through my long, wavy brunette hair and smack my lips intentionally, not making eye contact with him.

"You got laid." Finley squints from across the table, then smirks, knowing how much more fuel she's throwing on the fire for our father. He abhors us flaunting our sexuality.

"I really don't want to hear this." He tosses his hands in the air with a growl in his throat.

"Are you still leading Jack around like a little lost puppy dog while he pants all over you?" James squints, almost as if she's jealous.

"He's an idiot, but he's good in bed and gives me what I want." I flippantly shrug one shoulder and drum my shiny pink fingernails on the table.

"Did you girls not understand me when I said I didn't want to know about your sex lives?" Our father wags a stern finger at all three of us.

"Is that because you're not getting between some hot woman's thighs?" I can't hold back my snort and wait for him to lose his shit. Poking the bear is one thing; poking the judge takes on a whole new meaning.

"That's enough!" He slams his hand down on the table, and the rugged crease between his eyes deepens.

"Come on, Dad. You know we're just pulling your chain." Finley shuffles the papers in front of her neatly together. She's always been able to diffuse his temper. I have the opposite effect, sometimes intentionally.

Finley is a neat freak, unlike me. I don't care if things are in their place. "It's been twenty-four years since Mom died. I think she'd be okay if you moved on." As soon as the words leave my mouth, I instantly regret it when he almost breaks his neck twisting to glare daggers at me, pain searing his handsome face.

"You have no…"

I cut off his tongue-lashing. "I'm sorry. It's none of my business. I just hate to see you so lonely."

"I'm a solitary man, but I have you three girls, and that's enough for me." He exhales, and his face relaxes.

"What happens when one day we find someone to love, and we start lives of our own?" James asks, barely above a whisper.

She's got a point. Finley is an attorney and thirty-six years old. James is a thirty-four-year-old emergency room doctor, and she mentions having a child almost daily. She says her clock is ticking away for having babies.

The chances of any of us finding that certain someone is slim because of our side hustle. The old adage "looks can be deceiving" should truthfully be our family motto as opposed to "The Daughters of Judge Steel." We are all sophisticated, smart, and savvy in appearance. But in reality, we're all gritty, fractured savages living among the jungle of palm trees, led by our lion king, Benjamin Steel, aka Benny, when I really want to ruffle his mane. He's the creator of havoc in our daily grinds. Always searching for our next victim. It's his obsession, and he taught his lion cubs well. There will never be a normal for any of us, and some-times, I wonder what that would look like. *Boring comes to mind*. As screwed up as we all are, I love our lives. He worked hard to make his name as a judge in this town and paid for our college educa-tions with the money he took as a fee from his side hustle.

"You know that can never happen. We can't risk anyone knowing what we do. It would land us all in prison for a really long time, and I don't look good in stripes." He grips his middle daughter's shoulders.

James's head falls downward, and the disap-pointment is permanently etched in her pretty features. I reach over and squeeze her hand under the table. "When love finds you, we'll work it out," I say so only she can hear me. I've already put my

15

father in a mood. There's no need to egg him on more.

I often speculate what he was like before our mother died. I was only two, and at twenty-six, I don't have any memories of her. Only pictures and the locket I wear around my neck, holding her heartbeat. Finley was twelve and James ten when she took her last breath, and they both hold precious memories of her. I try to search my two-year-old mind, but I can't find her. Sometimes, I think I had it easier in comparison because I never knew our mother. My father frequently says I'm just like her. My sisters have always believed I'm his favorite because I remind him so much of our mother, the love of his life. It's strange to me how your personality can be like someone you were never around.

I possess her beautiful face, and I've learned to harness its power when necessary. When I first entered the realm of investment brokerage, predominantly dominated by men, I wasn't taken seriously. Men, both coworkers and clients, approached me with intentions that had little to do with investments. I proved myself a worthy opponent by carving my path in their domain by achieving my first multimillion-dollar deal with a company they had coveted for a long time. I was scrupulous, and I may or may not have used my looks and body to my advantage. They were going to believe what they wanted about me anyway, so I have no guilt, but what I do have is a sweet bank account. I could move anywhere in the world and live out my life peacefully, never working again, but my family means everything to me, and so does the judge's mission.

"Can we get on with this? I have to be in court in an hour." Finley hands each of us a folder.

Our father casually strolls around the table, looking over our shoulders as he speaks. "Our next job will be to teach Luther Craig a hard lesson. His photo is in your files."

"What's his sin?" I ask without flipping through the paperwork.

"He's an insurance agent who bilked our client, who is a mother of four, out of her husband's half-million-dollar insurance policy when he died suddenly."

"Bastard." I continue to tap my manicured nails on the table, already fantasizing about how good it's going to feel to bring him down a few notches and rob him blind. It gives me a better high than my uppers.

"Does he have a criminal background?" James asks while reading his bio.

"He's been in my court before, but his smooth-talking lawyer offered a settlement, then the son of a bitch filed bankruptcy and never paid out a dime."

"I'm sure his bankruptcy was fraudulent." I delve through my purse, searching for a bottle of pills.

My father's large hand lands on my collarbone, digging his fingertips in firmly. "I need you focused. The majority of this job will weigh on you." He leans close to my ears. "You don't need the pills, Audey."

At least he's not angry at me anymore. He's right. I don't need them, but I want the high. For now, I leave the pills in the bottom of my bag and peer up at him. "I'm paying attention."

"Good." He continues to circle the table as he speaks. "You'll make nice with him and swindle him into making a substantial investment."

"Judge." I roll my eyes dramatically like a child. "I hate being nice to scumbags."

He ignores me. "When he registers his investment with your firm, you'll hack his bank account."

"That sounds way too easy." James clicks the end of a pen.

"Famous last words," I huff. "Nothing is ever easy, and we're always at risk of getting caught."

"If you do, I know a good attorney." He winks at Finley.

"A judge too." James laughs.

"You'll set up a fake investment so that your company is not linked to it. He's a thief, but he's not stupid."

"Most of us thieves aren't." I slip my hand deep into my purse, opening the bottle, and when he looks the other way, I plant the little white tablet under my tongue.

James shoots me a sideways glance with a frown on her lips.

I lift both my shoulders toward my ears in response to her silent admonishment.

"You know the first rule. Don't get caught." Dad holds up a single finger.

"These photographs in the file show he has a safe in his bedroom." Finley slaps the picture onto the middle of the table.

"Sounds like the perfect job for Audrey. She's good at landing in a man's bedroom." James's tone is sarcastic as she looks away from me and at the papers in front of her.

I dislike that she thinks so little of me. Yes, I

could easily fall between the sheets with just about any man. I would never admit it to anyone, especially the judge, because he sees it as a weakness, but I fantasize that there's someone out there I could fall madly in love with, but I'd never expose a man to my reality. In my mind, there isn't a person alive who would understand what drives any of us and accept it for what we are. It keeps damage control at a minimum.

"I've included details of all his various bank accounts in Florida and two in the state of Nevada. It appears he likes to gamble, and he's pretty damn good at it. What I don't know is how much money he keeps in his safe." He places the palms of his hands on the table. "I want every red cent of it. We'll leave him with nothing."

"What's going to stop him from claiming bankruptcy again or starting over?" James scratches the side of her head.

"That's where Finley comes into play. You'll find a way to have his insurance license taken away, and any claims he makes will be addressed by his opposing attorney. If you bring him into my courtroom, he'll never stand a chance. Regardless if he attempts to claim bankruptcy again, we'll already own all his assets."

"What about me?" James asks. "What's my role in this plan?"

"The safe. You're the best at cracking them wide open."

"I do find them fascinating." A grin plays at the corner of her mouth as if she's really pleased with herself.

"Are we done?" I stand. "I could really use a dip in the pool."

"And I have to get to work." Finley scrapes the chair across the polished marble floor and neatly files her paperwork in her briefcase.

"I'm on night shift for the next week, so I'm going to bed." James kisses our father on the cheek and pads out of the dining room.

"Do you want to join me for an early swim?" I point at the pool through the sliding glass garage-style door that opens up to an immaculately kept deck overlooking the pool that faces the inlet.

"I can't." He breathes out. "I have to preside over a few cases today. I'm afraid it will be an extremely long day."

"How about I swing by later and bring you a coffee?" I'm not the sweet daughter I pretend to be; I have an ulterior motive. There's a sexy man working at the coffee shop that, by the looks of his mouth, I'd bet my life he'd be great in bed. Don't get me wrong, I love my father dearly, and I'd literally kill for him, but waiting on him or any man is not in my wheelhouse. I'm an independently wealthy woman who lives on adventure, and I admittedly have an addictive personality. One to drugs, two to sex. The dirtier, the better. Third, I love being a thief.

Drugs.

Sex.

Thief.

Quite the combination and a lot of appearances to keep up to hide in plain sight.

"If you could come around two, I'll have a break in my schedule. In the meantime, you need to study up on our current target."

"Have I ever let you down?" I step on my tiptoes, kissing his smooth, shaven face. "Love you, Judge."

"Love you too, angel." He laughs, knowing damn good and well I'm far from being angelic. I fight the devil perched on my shoulder daily.

Before I can walk away, his phone rings. He snatches me by the hand when he sees the number, narrowing his brown eyes with long strands of gray eyebrows dipping downward at me. He hits the speaker button and angles the phone for me to listen.

"Chief Carrington, what can I do for you?"

"Your daughter was speeding down North Ocean Drive again. She sent our new deputy on a chase, and he lost her. He described the vehicle, and there's only one like it in Palm Beach."

I scrunch my nose and raise a shoulder to my cheek. "You hate it when I'm late." I bat my lashes.

"Perhaps your department needs to purchase faster cars." He chuckles.

"Judge Steel—" he's cut off from finishing his sentence.

"I'll speak to her about it." He hangs up. "You stick out like a sore thumb in that damn yellow sports car. Try to keep the speeding to a minimum. I can only turn my back so many times."

"That's not true. You're the man of Steel. You can do anything." I wink.

Rushing to my room, I change into my skimpy red bikini and skip out of the house, diving into the deep end of the pool. In Florida, the water always feels like a warm bath in the middle of summer. I don't consider it refreshing, but I love the feel of it as I swim. Skimming over the water, swimming laps, my mind races. I always have a million questions streaming through my thoughts when I'm high. For instance, what would our lives be like if our mother was still alive? Would we still be in podunk Blackville, South Carolina, living in the single-wide trailer on a crappy piece of property?

We left there when I turned eight. Benny Steel went back to school after our mother died and spent every waking hour studying, leaving my sisters to raise me. A year after he became a lawyer, he won a big case that no one thought was possible, and he was elected by the governor to be a judge in this town. We took very little with us, and he torched the place on the way out. It was the first time that I can recollect him crying. Finley told me it was because he always dreamed of getting our mother out of our single wide and building her a home. I heard him say, "I couldn't do it for you, but I'm doing it for our girls. I'm so sorry, Violet." Then he loaded us up in our station wagon and never looked back. I'd bet my life on the fact that a day hasn't gone by since she hasn't lived in his mind.

He's been driven as long as I can remember, but my sisters remember being poorer than church mice. He attributes our mother's lack of care to the lack of money and blames the system for failing her, along with the medical staff. Everything he's done since then revolves around seeking retribution for those who have victimized the less fortunate.

He's dedicated countless hours grooming each of his daughters and happily involving us in his quest for vengeance. Surprisingly, we excel at it. Outwardly, we maintain an image of being prim and proper, but internally, we are a complex mix of emotions and experiences that most people would never understand. To put it plainly, we're all sorts of messed up.

There is nothing more rewarding than stealing from those who have wronged others and giving it back to their prey. I view my family as the contemporary equivalent of Robin Hood, with a twist. We understand that our actions are far from conventional, and it's possible that one day we'll face the consequences, but for now, it's a series of exhilarating adventures that bring us a unique sense of gratification. I know we are screwed up, and one day we'll likely be caught, but in the meantime, it's one big adventure after another, and it's very satisfying.

"There you are," Jack's voice has me jumping to the sound of it. "You left my bed again without saying a word."

I swim to the shallow end and sway my hips dramatically as I use the steps to get out. Water drips from my long hair down my lean body. "I'd think you'd be used to it by now." I trail my pointer finger over his chest and around to his back as my other hand unties the strings of my bikini bottoms. Typically, I'd kick his ass out for showing up here, but the drugs make me horny. I could either tend to it myself or let his rather lengthy dick tickle my fancy. I choose the latter, and he follows me into the house for a repeat of last night's raunchy sex.

Chapter 2
AUDREY

SHIMMING into my organic silk panties, I walk on my tiptoes to my bathroom and see Jack in the mirror, sitting on the edge of the bed. "You know I'm using you, right?" My tits jiggle when I flop my head over to brush my damp hair.

He stands, tugging on his jeans. "You tell me the same thing every time we fuck." He laughs. "Yet, you always end up in my arms."

I fling my head up and stand in the doorway. "I just want to make sure you know. I like you, but I can't have you falling in love with me."

He pads barefoot on the carpet and wraps his arms around me, fastening his hands to my ass. "It's a little too late for that. You know I love you."

"Then we can't screw around anymore."

"And you say that every time too." He kisses my cheek.

"I mean it this time."

"Until you're high again, and then my phone rings."

I push free of him. "I mean it."

"Then why do you keep showing up on my doorstep?"

"Because I like the way you screw, but I'm not nor will I ever be in love with you, Jack."

"I'll wait around until you change your mind."

I softly swat his cheek. "I won't. And next time you show up at my house unannounced, I'll cut your balls off. You're lucky my father had already left the property."

"Yeah, the only person that scares me more than you is Judge Benny."

"Judge Steel to you." I jab a finger in his finely haired chest.

"Why do you have to be so damn difficult?" He picks up his shirt where I threw it when I stripped it off his body. "And rough." He points to a rip in his T-shirt.

"You like it that way, and you know it," I huff. "As far as me being a handful, that won't change either." I walk into my closet and push hanger after hanger of expensive clothes to the side until I find the perfect dress.

He sits on the bench at the end of my bed and jerks on his shoes. "You have a sweet side you like to hide."

"There is nothing sweet about me." The dress slips easily over my head and down my C-cup bare breasts.

"I didn't say you didn't have to look really hard to see it." He grins, stands, and makes his way over to me. "You look pretty."

"Thanks, but I need you to get the hell out of here." I march past him, slipping my heels back on in the bathroom. Pulling open a drawer, I apply a light sheen of makeup.

"You don't need that crap. You're a natural beauty. And that mole above your top lip is sexy as hell."

"Are you still here?" I scowl at him in the mirror.

He smacks me on the ass. "You know where to find me when you need your itch scratched. I'll catch you later, Audrey." He waves and finally walks out.

I sigh deeply. "Why am I so messed up?" I stare at my reflection. He's not a terrible guy, but he's not exactly my type, although he's good in bed. If I can't have the fictional man of my dreams, I still need sex, and usually, I limit my escapades with Jack. There are occasional exceptions, like the times I pick up a guy in a bar when I'm in a drugged haze, as that seems to be when my sexual impulses intensify the most. Opening a drawer, I pick up a pill bottle. "I should give you up." Instead of tossing it in the trash or flushing it down the toilet, I throw it back in the drawer and stare at the mole above my lip. I used to hate its existence until I recognized the same blemish on my mother in a picture of her at my age. Now I cherish it. I have no other marks on my skin, no freckles or sunspots, just the mole.

Finishing my makeup with a soft pink lip shade, I snag my cell phone, stuff it in my purse, and hook my keys on my fingers. Before I make it out of my bedroom, my Maine Coon cat sprawls out on the floor, wanting her belly rubbed.

Meow, she purrs.

"How come you always wait until Jack leaves to show up." I gather her in my arms. "You don't like him, do you, Shambles?" I scratch her chin, and her motor gets louder. Her name is appropriate for how I feel about my life. Chaotic, but by outward appearances, put together. She belonged to one of our victims who solely used her for breeding and kept her locked in a cage. She found herself tied and shoved in a small kennel, unable to move. James took pity on her pleas and released her after a day or so. I have no tolerance for anyone who mistreats animals. She's my confidant, my secret keeper, and I'd kill anyone who tried to harm her.

Backing out of the garage and making a half-circle loop in the driveway, I see a cop car parked at the end where the winding concrete meets the pavement. I honk the horn and wave, pulling onto Ocean Drive. The wild part of me wants to lay my foot on the gas pedal until it hits the floor. Instead, I drive the speed limit into town, ending my journey at the Bond & Bevel Coffee House. I love the name of the business. The place used to be a small bank, and there's a vault the owner, who I've yet to meet, uses as his office and creates leather products out of it. It's totally a man's man coffee house, complete with an assortment of axes and knives mounted on the walls. It sells high-end humidors, Italian cigar clippers, rectangle marble cigar ashtrays, and various handmade leather items.

From what I've seen, the owner has worked hard to get the place remodeled, having the majority of the work done at night. I've only seen him from the backside leaving my father's chamber, hand delivering coffee and a variety of bagels to his office. According to my father, they became fast friends, which is odd for the judge. He rarely takes the time to get to know anyone. He's told me they've hung out together on occasion. My father is tight-lipped, and I'm sure the guy doesn't know anything outside the fact that my father is a judge.

The wildly hot guy behind the counter sees me as soon as I prance through the door. He excuses himself from a customer, swaggering in my direction, smiling that perfect smile of his that first caught my attention. His sharp green eyes twinkle off his black shoulder-length curly hair. He rolls up his sleeves as he comes closer, and my sex drive roars to life even though it hasn't even been an hour since I was screwing Jack's brains out.

"Hey, beautiful," he says, lightly kissing my cheek.

"Business appears to be good." I point at the line of customers.

"It's been busy all week. Did you come by to pick up an order? Since you haven't told me your name, I don't know if it's ready or not." He twirls a tendril of my hair between this pointer finger and thumb. "You have a disadvantage knowing mine." His gaze dips to the name tag on his company shirt.

"Audrey." I extend my hand.

"Thomas," he says, kissing my knuckles.

I can already tell he's going to be way too sweet for me. "I didn't place an order yet."

"A man couldn't have been so lucky thinking you'd dropped in to see him." He chuckles.

Okay, good-looking and a mouth that promises pleasure, but too clingy. "I promised my father I'd bring him a coffee because he's going to be at the courthouse all day."

"Throw in a couple of muffins for her," he tells the barista, and she rolls her eyes at him, obviously jealous he's paying attention to me. "May I walk with you to your father's office?"

"This place is crazy busy."

"I can take a break."

"Perhaps another time." I purse my lips, wanting him to take the hint that I've changed my mind. *Why? Because he kissed my hand? I'm so damaged.*

He meanders behind the counter, prepares the coffee himself, and removes two blueberry muffins from the glass case, putting them inside a paper bag with the coffee house's logo on it. "Anything else?" he asks. His grin is gone.

"That will do. Thank you." I'm hot one minute and cold the next. All he did was kiss the back of my hand, and the simple, sweet gesture turned me off. *I need way more therapy.*

I walk through the metal detectors and take the

elevator to the third floor. Knocking, I open the door with my free hand. "Hey, Dad."

He peers up over his thick, black-rimmed glasses. "I've been looking forward to a good cup of joe since you mentioned it this morning." He gets to his feet and kisses my cheek, taking his coffee from me. "What's in the bag that smells so good?"

"Blueberry muffins." I toss them on his desk.

"Did you meet Rhett?"

"Is that the new owner?"

"Yes. He's a great guy."

"That says a lot coming from you." I take the seat opposite his massive dark pecan-stained desk. "But no, I've yet to meet him. Is he my type?" I waggle my brows.

"No man is your type, Audey." He chuckles before he blows on his coffee. "You eat them all alive."

"Tell me about him?" I prop my heels on his desk, and he grunts.

"He's twenty years older than you, and I've already told you he's a good guy. He's off-limits to you." He aims a finger at me, speaking in his judge voice. "We play golf together on Fridays."

"You should invite him over for dinner. I'll cook."

"No," he simply states and sips his coffee.

"Suit yourself." I shrug.

"Have you made contact with Luther Craig?"

"I've been a little busy. I'll work on it when I leave here."

"I'll expect an update as soon as you do."

"You know, I do have a life and a real job of my own." I get a little snarky with him.

"Dare I ask what you did after your swim?"

My eyes narrow.

"You know we have cameras all over the house. Tell Jack if he wanders onto my property again, I'll have him arrested for trespassing."

"He's harmless."

"Anyone visiting our house is a potential danger to our family."

"It would be nice to act like an ordinary family and have friends over every now and then." I fold my arms over my chest. "What do you and Rhett chat about when you're golfing?"

"I'm very careful what I say around him."

"What do you think he would do if he knew we were thieves?"

"I'm not about to find out. You need to focus on your job."

"What if I just want a normal life?"

"You'd be bored, and you know it." He half laughs with a smirk.

"What if I want to fall in love like you did with my mom?"

"I'm trying to protect you. Love will only leave you brokenhearted."

"Mom died. She didn't leave you."

"She was murdered, as far as I'm concerned," he growls.

"And you made them all pay for it. You single-handedly shut down the men on the board at the hospital, and the facility went under. The doctor that cared for her had his license taken away on false charges you conjured up. Isn't that enough?"

"You didn't mention the millions we stole from him. And no, it's never enough. I don't want anyone to ever be at the mercy of someone else because of money. It's my life's mission to take every one of them down."

I inhale, get to my feet, walk around the desk, and kiss him on the cheek. "I love you, Dad. Don't ever quit being you because I whine a bit. I believe in what we're doing. I only wish it wasn't a lonely world."

"I'm sorry, angel, but that's the way it has to be."

Chapter 3
♥ AUDREY

"LUTHER CRAIG," I mutter, flipping the pages of his file and bring up a Google search on him. He's got a LinkedIn profile with his mug on it. "Fifty years old, been in the insurance business for ten years. What did you do prior to that, Luther?" Another search shows him living in Las Vegas. "That explains the two bank accounts in Nevada." He moved here the same time he started his insurance business. Divorced, father of two boys. His ex-wife's name is listed, and I look her up on Facebook. It's amazing what you can find out when you've scorned a woman.

She rants to one of her friends that he was accused of embezzling money from the auto parts store he was keeping the books for, but it was never proven. Looks like he smacked her around a few times too. I enlarge the picture of his wife's face with bruises on it.

"It will give me great pleasure to rob you blind and ruin your life." She blatantly states he isn't paying her child support either. I'll verify that when I hack into his accounts. "If he's not supporting his kids, they'll get a big bonus at the end of this job," I mumble to myself. She also mentions he joined Gamblers Anonymous as part of his custody agreement for his boys. He never attended, so she refused to let him see his kids.

"Sounds like your gambling is a priority over your children." I tap the keys hard because it pisses me off. People like him shouldn't be allowed to be a parent. Sadly, the ones that want to be die when they have young children. At least in my world, that's the reality.

I sit back in my chair and twist a pen between my fingers. "So what could I lure you in with, Mr. Loser?"

"Crypto." I snap. "I'll create a fake coin and entice him with it. It's the perfect investment for a gambler." It will take a bit of work to set it all up to make it look real. I can have Finley assist me with the legalities to make it look like an up-and-coming marketable coin.

"Hey." Finley peeks in my office.

"Speak of the devil, and she appears," I snort.

"Dad's not home yet?"

"It's not my night to keep tabs on him, but I'm

betting he hit a bar. He always does when it gets close to the anniversary of our mother's death."

"Dang, you're right. It is that time of year." She strolls into the office and checks out the pictures hanging on the walls. "I still can't believe you jumped out of a plane. You're a lot braver than me."

"It was exhilarating."

"I'd almost forgotten about your illegal drag racing," she roars, pointing at the picture.

"That was fun too. I was higher than a kite."

"Dad was so mad he let you stew in jail for the night."

"Yeah, he was pretty red-faced about it. He threatened to have my driver's license revoked."

"Are you working on Luther Craig's file?" She finally sits.

"Yes, and I think I've come up with a good plan. He's a gambler and a deadbeat father."

"Oh, I know how much that irks you." She scrunches her nose.

"He smacked his wife around a few times, too, so this will be fun. I want to create a fake crypto coin and sell him on it. The selling will be the easy part. Setting it up will be a challenge, and that's where you come in. I'll need legal terms to make it look legit."

"Once you have it in place, I'll gladly look over it. I found something buried on him. He had his insurance license years ago, and it was revoked in Nevada."

"His wife claims he was embezzling money from the company he worked for."

"I'm betting our client isn't the only one he swindled. If I can prove it, not only will he never be able to sell insurance again, he'll be behind bars."

"It's where the asshole belongs as far as I'm concerned, and the four of us are going to ensure he gets there in due time and leave him with nothing but his balls. He won't even have toilet paper to wipe his ass."

"You're pretty ruthless," she snickers.

"Can I ask you something?"

"Anything."

"I know Dad has told me what our mother was like, but I'd like to know your thoughts. We've never really discussed it because it upsets Dad."

"She was beautiful, like you. You have her exact same steely green eyes. I remember thinking she was larger than life. Very adventurous, yet she had a sweet innocence about her that none of us inherited."

"That's not true. James is sweet, and Jack accused me of hiding my sweetness."

"Ha! What did you say to that?"

"I basically told him to rot in hell." I laugh.

"She transformed our father. He had a rough upbringing, growing up as a poor kid left to fend for himself while his mother worked tirelessly to support him after his father abandoned them. He was headed down a dark path, tangled in drugs and violence. He often mentioned how our mother saw something in him that he couldn't see in himself. She, he told me, was the catalyst for his profound change. He became an exemplary husband and a devoted father, cherishing our mother and revering every step she took. He made a solemn promise to her, vowing to lift her out of the trailer park they lived in. He worked tirelessly at a factory, juggling night classes as he pursued a better future. However, when her illness first surfaced, he had to quit school and began searching for a second job. In Blackville, one of the nation's poorest towns, he was fortunate to have the job he did. But as her condition worsened, he missed more work, and the company terminated his employment, leading to the loss of both his insurance and income."

"How did I not know any of this?"

"You were just six months old when it happened."

"I wish sometimes he'd find someone else to fall in love with so he'd let go of the chaos he lives with, and then maybe we could all have a regular life."

"I do, too, but I don't think that's going to happen."

"Don't you ever get lonely?"

"Of course I do, but this is my lot in life. It wasn't any different being a teenager and trying to tend to you. Dad was back in school, and I had to sacrifice my life to raise you."

I reach over the desk and place my hand on hers. "I'm sorry."

"It wasn't your fault, and I'm not complaining. I'm just accepting that my place will always be needed here at home."

"I want more than that for you. Why don't you get a place of your own and stop working his game? You're a successful attorney. You don't need this crap."

"Neither do you, but here we are, and I tend to think you enjoy it."

"I think it's an illness," I scoff.

"I do wish you'd get help with your addictions. I don't want to come home to find you dead one day."

"It's nothing I can't control." Yes, I'm in complete denial.

"Just let me know what you need for the crypto coin. I'm going to bed. It's been a long day."

I shut my computer down. "I'm going to go check on the judge. There's only one place he goes to drown his sorrows."

"Let me know if you don't find him."

"Good night." I snatch my keys and hold my phone to my ear with my shoulder as I climb into my car. I call his phone, and it goes straight to voicemail.

At a stoplight, I poke through my purse, grabbing a bottle of pills. I shake it. "Empty." Opening the center console, I find one pill that spilled out in the bottom of it. "Thank god." I pop it in my mouth and swallow it dry, then tap the gas pedal when the light turns green, spinning my tires.

Dad's Escalade is the first vehicle I recognize in the parking lot. "Hey, Jay," I speak to the bouncer.

"He's inside." He hikes a thumb over his shoulder, holding the door open for me.

"Thanks."

I scan the dim room and spot him at the end of the bar, sitting in front of an empty bottle of Wild Turkey. It's cheap crap, but it's his favorite.

"Judge," I say, leaning on the bar next to him.

His eyes are glassed over when he snarls. "What the hell are you doing here? This is a private party." His hand wobbles when he picks up his last sip of bourbon whiskey.

"I think you've had enough. Let me drive you home."

"I'm not ready to leave," he slurs.

"Then how about I have a drink with you." I tap my knuckles on the shiny wooden bar and order straight tequila. My drugs kick in, and I'm feeling no pain.

"To the memory of Violet." He clinks my glass with his empty one. "She was a damn good woman." His eyes mist over even after all these years.

"She gave you three smart, gorgeous daughters."

Dad spins in his chair to face me. "Yes, she did, but you"—he touches my nose—"will be the death of me. You're so much like your mother it hurts."

Thus, the reason I take drugs. I can't stand the thought of hurting him just by my presence. "Please let me take you home. I don't think a judge needs to be seen out in public drinking, much less driving."

"I'm not riding in that thing you call a car," he stammers and wavers when he stands.

He's got a point. At six feet three, he'd have to

fold in half to get inside. "I'll drive yours and come back to get mine."

"Try not to piss off the cops in my Escalade," Dad slurs again and damn near falls flat on his face, walking on the gravel parking lot.

"That's all we need. A visit to the emergency room. At least if you hit your head, James is on duty."

He stumbles again before he makes it inside the vehicle.

I hustle to the driver's side before my father decides to get out and have another drink. I drive the speed limit home out of respect for him, and I practically drag him inside the house because he's so out of it.

After pulling off his shoes, I attempt to remove his belt and fail when he passes out cold on his back.

"Are you trying to wake the dead?" Finley yawns from his doorway.

"Sorry. Help me get him in bed. You lift his legs, I'll get his shoulders."

He's tall and solid, and we struggle to get him situated.

"This used to be mine and James's job," she whispers. "It happened a lot after our mother died."

She leans down, kissing him on the forehead. "He's going to be grumpy in the morning."

"He's grumpy most days," I say, stepping out of his bedroom with her. "Did you know that he and the owner of the coffee shop play golf together?"

"Yeah, he's mentioned it."

"Have you met him?"

"He brings Dad coffee to the courthouse."

"What's he like?"

"Why are you so curious?" She drapes her arm over my shoulder.

"I guess I'm just not used to the judge making friends. I want to protect him like he does us."

She yawns again. "I can tell you this, he's not bad on the eyes."

"Has anyone done a background check on him?"

"You worry too much. And you're sounding way too much like our old man. Good night, little sis." She waves and shuts the door to her room.

"He did a background check on my high school boyfriend," I mutter and pad to my room, flopping on the bed.

Chapter 4
AUDREY

SLEEP HAS NEVER BEEN my friend, and I refuse to take downers due to the unwanted side effects of poor concentration. I always have to be on my game. The uppers, though they make most people anxious, make me feel more alive, invincible, and there's the added pleasure of horniness. They make me a tad bit ADHD, but I do my best work when I'm high. My brain races to new heights with all sorts of ideas.

I dressed in a gray pencil skirt, a soft rose-colored blouse, and shiny black closed-toe heels for a rare day at the office. Most of my work I do ocean-side, sipping on a frozen mango margarita or two, sometimes three, depending on how well my day is going.

All stares are on me when I stroll through the office door, slinging my hair over my shoulder and removing my round-framed Gold and Wood sunglasses, tucking them inside the pocket of my purse.

"Well, look what the cat dragged in." Colin Prath's, the owner of the investment firm, gaze skims down my long legs.

"Good morning." I plaster on my fake smile and make a conscious effort not to grind my teeth.

He glances at his black matte Rolex. "It's almost noon, Ms. Steel."

"I've already accomplished days' worth of work before you even got out of bed this morning," I boast. He's married to a woman he considers a mere trophy. He's been involved with nearly every secretary who has worked at the firm, and it's been a constant rotation of women. Colin, in particular, made unwelcome advances, attempting to breach my personal space more than once until I put him in his place, almost breaking his pinky finger.

"According to the numbers I've seen in the latest report, you've had a good month."

"You mean a damn good year." My heels click on the pristine flooring as I make my way to my coveted corner office.

He follows me. "You really should check in more often. I have men dying to get their hands on this space. If you're not going to use it, I'm tempted to give it to one of them."

"You'll do no such thing. As long as I bring in

twice the money as everyone else, this place is mine regardless of whether I use it or not." I point my finger to the floor.

He lifts his hand to his mouth, tapping a finger on his lip. "I'll hold them off for now, but I would like you to be here more often."

After placing my bag into the bottom drawer of my desk, I smooth my skirt beneath me and sit in my Italian leather chair. "For what purpose? I work better elsewhere with no distractions." My lips flatten, smearing my gloss.

He plops down in the chair across from my desk, bracing his hands behind his head with his elbows wide. "I like it when you're in the office. I get tired of dealing with these young men vying to make a name for themselves."

"We've all been there, Colin, or have you forgotten?" I raise a brow.

"That's what makes you so different." He takes his hands from behind his head and presses his palms on my desk. "You walked in knowing you'd win and did it within weeks. These candy-ass graduates don't know their elbow from their assholes."

"It's your job to mentor them." I tap the button, turning on my computer.

"I'll pay you a salary to do it for me."

I laugh. "Not going to happen. I make more money in an hour than most people make in an entire year."

"Then do it because I'm asking you to. There isn't anyone better at this job than you, other than me." He rests back, crossing one leg over the other at the knee and clasping his hands together on his lap.

"You're wrong. I'm better than you, and you know it."

"You just might be." He chuckles. "What are you working on? Or should I ask about a specific investment that has caught your eye?" He tries to peek at my screen, but I angle it away from his view.

"Do your own research."

"You could be a team player and share."

"I tried that once, and you screwed me over, so no thanks. Don't you have a secretary to mess around with or something?"

"You are out of the loop. I gave up extramarital affairs." He uncomfortably adjusts his tie.

My eyes pop wide open, and I grin. "You finally got caught."

"Yes, and it's cost me dearly. Imagine my pain going to couples' therapy." His lip raises.

"Ha. Serves you right. I warned you one day

she'd find out. I'm surprised your wife is giving you a second chance. She's way too good for you."

"Ouch." He feigns hurt, laying his hand over his heart. "This coming from the woman who thinks she's untouchable." He leans forward. "I'd give her up for you. Just say the word."

"Do I need to break your finger this time?" I give him a sideways glance.

He tucks his pinky into his other hand. "A man can dream."

"Not about me. I don't ever mix business with pleasure." When I first laid eyes on Colin, I thought he was gorgeous until he opened his arrogant mouth. He's tall, broad-shouldered, square-chinned, and has deep, dark blue eyes. The kind of man in the leading roles in movies, but definitely not my type.

What is my type?

Not Jack.

Not Colin, and not the hot guy at the coffee shop.

"All business," he mumbles with disappointment in his eyes. "Seriously, would you at least consider running a few in-house training classes?"

"That I can do. I'll write down specific target points and send them to you for your approval."

"I'm sure whatever you have to teach them will

be beneficial." He remains seated, poking his tongue to the side of his mouth, making it protrude.

"Is there something else?"

He stands, rubbing the creases from his slacks. "Just keep working your magic and bringing in the big accounts."

"I have a dinner meeting set up with the owner of Brown Industries. He has a few million dollars he's looking to invest."

"Damn, how did you swing a meeting with him?" He cocks a brow.

"He sought me out. He'd heard about my successful investments through a colleague of his and called me for a meeting."

"When is it?"

"Tonight."

"Would you mind if I tagged along?"

"I would mind. A lot." My fake smile is back in place. "He very specifically asked that I not bring you. Seems one of his nieces was a temporary secretary at the front desk, and she didn't speak to kindly of you. I'm amazed that he'll even consider doing business with your firm."

"I'll be sure to steer clear. Schmooze him, and give him whatever he wants." His gaze falls to my breasts.

"Why do you assume that my body is part of the deal?" I snap.

"You're right. I'm sorry." He holds his hands out in surrender. "You're highly intelligent and very professional when it comes to your job, and I respect you for it, regardless of what some others might think."

"Let them believe what they want. They are just jealous."

He takes large strides to the door. "You have to admit, your beauty doesn't hurt a bit."

"My appearance plays no role in sealing a deal. I excel at my research, and my clients reap the benefits of my investment expertise, not from my personal involvement with them. If you could kindly proceed toward the exit, I have a substantial workload ahead of me as I prepare for my upcoming meeting."

He salutes me. "Make me some money."

"Jerk." I grind my teeth when he's out of my office.

I spend the next several hours collecting data for my meeting and then turn my attention to Luther Craig, our new prey. I take my time researching newly released crypto coins in the market. I mark the positives, which ones ticked upward when they hit the market, and if they continued to rise or dipped after their initial release. I combine their attributes to form a plan. Checking the time, I need to skate out and get ready for my meeting. Daryl Brown let me choose the spot, and it just so happens to be the same place where Luther Craig can be found on a Friday night.

Turning off my computer, I snag my bag and lock my office door, then slip off my shoes to take the two flights of stairs to the ground floor. There's a middle-aged man walking circles around my car. He stops when he sees me with my keys clutched in my hand.

"Is this yours?"

"Yes."

"Sweet ride. It must have cost you a fortune. What do you do for a living?"

I point to the investment broker sign.

"You must be damn good. I've got a few pennies to spare. Perhaps you could give me your business card." He walks a few feet from me.

"I don't deal in pennies." I laugh.

"Obviously not." He chuckles, and a blush of pink covers his cheeks.

Pursing my lips, I take out my wallet and hand

him a business card. "I can turn your pennies into gold."

He tucks the card into the pocket of his shirt. "I'll give you a call. Thank you." He does an about-face and walks across the street.

"See, you were worth it. Your looks are going to make me even richer." I pat the hood of my car and then climb inside. Making a quick stop at the bank before it closes, I zoom into the parking lot and run inside. The manager always stops what he's doing when he sees me.

"Ms. Steel." He offers me his hand.

"Tim." I shake it. "I need to shuffle some funds to my charity."

"I can handle that for you." He leads me to his office. "Your cancer charity foundation has aided so many people. You should be very proud of yourself." He sits, tapping his keyboard. "How much do you want to add to it?"

I take out my phone and quickly calculate what I've earned this month from the investment firm. "Two million." I shift half of what I make into the foundation.

"That's very generous of you. May I ask you something?"

"Of course."

"Why do you keep your foundation anonymous? The world should know what you do for them."

"I don't believe in tooting my own horn." The real reason is that if I'm ever put in prison for my misgivings, the foundation will continue without being connected to me in any way. Finley made sure of it, and she's bound to secrecy because no one else knows about it.

"So, you won't be showing your face at the charity gala when they write the check for the cancer wing?"

"Oh, I'll be there. I just won't be center stage." I stand. "Are we done here?"

"Yes, I believe so." He taps one final key.

"Thank you, as always, for your discretion."

He gets up. "Happy to be of service, Ms. Steel."

I nod, heading out of the glass doors back to my car. "Screw it," I mutter and lay on the gas pedal, speeding down Ocean Drive, not caring if I'm chased or not. My tires squeal when I make the turn into our driveway. The judge is watering the flowers around the fountain in the middle of the circular drive. He refuses to hire anyone to take care of the property. Not because he can't afford it. He keeps this place secluded from the world, and he says the flowers remind him of my mother. He has blue violets dotting the property and has them regularly shipped to the house all year round.

"You keep driving like that, and you're going to wrap yourself around a pole," he grumbles when I step out of the car.

"I'm a good driver." Shutting the door, I walk over to where he's standing.

"Did you make any headway on our target?"

"I've come up with a plan to draw him in, but it's going to take time to work out the specific details. It's complicated."

"Will it work?" He raises a single gray brow.

"Yes. With Finley's help, I'm sure of it."

"Why are you in such a hurry, angel?"

"I've got a meeting with a potential client, and it just so happens to be at the same restaurant where Luther can be found on a Friday night."

"You want to see how he operates in public." It's not a question; he knows my MO.

"A chance meeting can't hurt. Or a stolen cell phone." I grin.

"Smart girl. Just don't get caught."

"I'll leave you with your flowers on a Friday night." I can't keep the sarcasm or the smirk off my lips.

"Don't start with me, Audey."

"Fine. I'll get laid twice to cover what you're missing out on."

"You know, you're always supposed to love your children, but I don't have to like you." He throws me some serious side-eye.

"I'll see you in the morning. Have fun with your violets." I rush off before he unleashes his wrath.

"Hey, girl." I rub Shambles between her ears, and she gets up from her sunny spot, trotting up the stairs behind me to my room.

"*Meow*."

"I can only hold you for a minute." I bend down, picking her up. "You need to quit catching so many mice. You're getting heavy." I cradle her under her hind legs, and she nuzzles her nose under my neck as I carry her into my closet to find the perfect outfit for tonight. Nothing low cut. I want professional, yet something I can peel out of to get Luther's attention.

"What do you think about this one, Shambles?" I hold up a white silk blouse and a pair of navy slacks.

"*Meow*," she mewls again.

"I think so too." My grip grows firmer around her when I step on my tiptoes to reach a shoe box on the top shelf. I haven't worn them before, and they'd be perfect with my outfit.

"Crap," I say when the box next to it falls down,

scaring Shambles. She lunges out of my arms. "Sorry, girl." I squat to pick up the contents of the box and see the letter from my mother. The envelope has remained sealed after all these years. I've never gotten up the nerve to open it. I imagine it's her final goodbye to me and all sorts of well wishes for my future, but I can't bear to open it. Instead, I clutch the beating locket around my neck and feel her heart beating. "You'd be disappointed in the things I've done," I whisper and stuff the letter back in the box and tuck it away.

Chapter 5
♥ AUDREY

THE MEAT MARKET Steakhouse is the busiest and most expensive restaurant in Palm Beach. Luther Craig is living high off the hog with other people's money. Stealing from others has made him a wealthy man. I realize the irony of a thief calling out a thief, but none of my money has come from the pure pleasure of making people pay for their sins.

Mr. Brown, though rich, is more of a down-to-earth kind of guy, and he might find the restaurant a bit pretentious until he sinks his teeth into the steak and lobster.

I arrived early to watch Luther, who is sitting at the end of the bar with two women. Four barstools down from his, I take the empty seat so I can hear his conversation. He's not bad-looking, but too thin for my liking. He has that boy next door vibe going on, and I can see why women would like him. Luther is undoubtedly a skilled conversationist, effortlessly weaving a web of charm and charisma.

"What can I get you?" The bartender places a small white napkin in front of me.

"Grey Goose on the rocks." I need a stiff drink if I'm going to have to play nice with Luther.

"And you?" he asks whoever pulled out the barstool next to mine.

"Three fingers of Wild Turkey." His drink of choice and scruffy Kevin Costner voice has me spinning toward him. I stare at him with my mouth gaping.

"Hello," he greets me with a warm smile, and in that moment, it feels like my entire world tilts on its axis. He is, without a doubt, the most striking man I've ever encountered—ruggedly handsome and exuding a timeless charm. I estimate him to be about two decades older than me. His hair, a lovely shade of light brown, carries hints of silver around his temples and sprinkled within his closely trimmed beard. His mustache retains the same soft, inviting, light brown hue as the rest of his hair. His deep, entrancing eyes, a shade reminiscent of rich milk chocolate, captivate me completely. It's safe to say that milk chocolate has just become my new favorite color. Above his right eyebrow, there's a distinct J-shaped scar that accentuates the wrinkles around the curve of his eye. Four gentle, well-defined lines grace his forehead, adding character to his demeanor.

"Do I have something on my face?" he asks, wiping his mouth with his left hand that bears no wedding ring.

"I'm sorry...I..." *Why am I tongue-tied?* I've spoken to powerful men with no hesitation, and yet, I sit in front of this man who's wearing a soft white long-sleeved T-shirt and an everyday pair of jeans that fit him perfectly. His shoes even enhance his good looks. *Lord, I'd love to see him barefoot.*

"I have a friend that always orders Wild Turkey," I finally find my voice even though I didn't say anything clever.

His lip curls up slightly, not a full-on smile but a gesture of amusement, and I can't help but think that my inner desires have burst into a sultry serenade, playing a few notes from the seductive melody from the song "Wicked Games."

"I have one of those friends too."

"Cheap crap, but he says it goes down smooth."

"That it does." The bartender slides both of our drinks in front of us.

"Are you here on business or pleasure?" He clinks his glass with mine.

A longing pulses through my core, and I find

myself yearning to cancel tonight's plans and indulge in some enjoyment with this captivating stranger who's left my stomach tied in knots. It's as if he possesses some enchanting power, for I feel utterly spellbound.

"Whoever you're meeting is a lucky man." His appreciative gaze takes a leisurely stroll down to my feet.

"Likewise." I bite the corner of my lip. What's amazing is that I have no drugs on board, and I'm totally turned on by him.

"My name is..."

"No, don't tell me." I laugh, placing my hand over his mouth. I feel his soft whiskers in the palm of my hand. "The next time we meet, you can tell me."

"Is that your way of asking me out on a date?"

I brazenly graze his temple with my fingers, thinking he could be a window into a normal life. His scent is intoxicating. I've never asked a man out before. "Would you say yes if I did?"

He shifts to the edge of his seat, and his milk chocolate eyes bore into mine. "It depends." His gentle breath caresses my skin with warmth.

I smile so hard my mouth hurts. My focus slides to his perfect mouth. "On what?"

"Are you married?"

"God no." I laugh, throwing my head back.

"Do you have a boyfriend?"

"Um, that would be a no too." I'm practically gasping for breath.

"Are you going to break my heart?" He tilts his head to the side, and there's a hint of vulnerability in his voice.

I'm good at lying, but why does the truth fly off my tongue. "Yes, that is likely what would happen."

He studies me for a long moment, and I could swear everything around us goes silent, but the silence between us roars loud. "Honest. I like that." He quirks one corner of his mouth.

"I haven't seen you in here before. Are you new in town or just enjoying the atmosphere and food?"

"I moved here six months ago from Boston."

"Funny, I didn't pick up on a Northeastern accent."

"That's because I don't have one. I was born and raised in Tampa. I moved to Boston to coach hockey when I left the military."

"What brought you back to Florida?"

"Semi-retirement." He laughs. "That didn't work out so well for me."

"Oh, didn't like the stillness?" I sip my drink, wanting to take him in.

"Boredom doesn't look good on me. I bought a coffee shop, and I'm coaching a group of teen boys at the ice rink."

Coffee shop? "I love coffee."

"You should come by the Bond and Bevel sometime."

Rhett, my father's friend. I remember Finley mentioning that he was rather easy on the eyes, and she certainly wasn't mistaken. "It depends," I playfully retort, and he responds with a flash of his impeccably straight, perfect white teeth, much like the rest of him.

"On what?"

"Are you married?"

His grin grows bigger. "No."

"A girlfriend?" I lift a brow.

"No."

"Will you break my heart?"

He inhales deeply. "Never."

"Then I just may have to take you up on it." I down the rest of my drink, throw cash on the counter, and stand. I give my thighs a quick shake to help my pants legs to straighten.

"Wait." He places his hand on my forearm, and I

love the feel of his touch. "I don't know anything about you. If you won't tell me your name, at least tell me what you do for a living so I might find you again."

I lick my lips, deciding against revealing that he's one of my father's acquaintances. "I'm a thief and a bit of a troublemaker." I wink and sashay my hips to the table where Daryl Brown has just been seated by the hostess. Glancing over my shoulder, Rhett is nibbling on his lower lip, a hint of a smile playing on his face, and his gaze fixed on my behind. I can't help but wish I could set aside my responsibilities to spend more time with him. The silver lining is I know precisely where I can locate him.

"Good evening." I walk over and shake my soon-to-be client's hand.

"Prompt, I like it," he says, pulling my chair out for me.

"Thank you." I sit.

"This is quite the restaurant." He takes the seat across from me and places the linen napkin in his lap.

"It's the best, and you're going to love the food."

The waiter takes our order and Daryl retrieves a pen and a notebook from his briefcase. "I hope you don't mind. I'm old school."

"Not at all. I take notes all the time." I fold my hands on the table, ready for any questions he fires at me. I've memorized all the specifics of the investment I'm proposing to him.

He asks, and I answer all of his questions in detail without hesitation. Our food comes, and it distracts him long enough for me to look for two people. Rhett, whose chair has been vacated, and Luther, who hasn't moved an inch.

"I'm very impressed with you, Ms. Steel. I've loaded you with question after question, and I scratched down your answers, but you never once had to look anything up."

"I'm always fully prepared when it comes to my clients, Mr. Brown."

"Daryl, please." He smiles with his mouth closed.

"I can guarantee that if you invest with me, you'll be more than happy with your return."

"From your reputation, I have no doubts, and after meeting with you, I'm more sure than ever. Let's enjoy our meal, and I'll sign the paperwork after dessert."

I like him. He's a family man and wants to leave his legacy to his grandchildren. When he talks about them, they bring pure joy to his features. He's proud of each and every one of them. It makes me wonder what I'd be like if he were my father. I know the judge loves me, but he's a harsh man, and he wasn't easy on any of us. He expected perfection, but his twisted mind held us captive, never free to make our own choices. I've always done what was expected of me, just like my sisters. He chose our careers based on what would benefit the family. A lawyer to keep us out of trouble. A doctor not only to treat our wounds but to gain access to the health care system to rob it blind, and an investment broker to invest and hide the money. I never got the chance to dream about what I wanted to be when I grew up.

We finish our cheesecake, and I take my tablet from my purse and bring up the contract.

"I have to admit. You were right about this place. Pretentious, but the food was well worth it." He electronically signs on the bottom line. "I'll have funds dispersed first thing in the morning."

"I'll email you when everything is set up. You'll get a weekly update from me with your return on investment."

"I'm trusting it will be substantial."

"I think you'll be very pleased." I tuck the tablet back into my bag.

He glances at his watch. "If you'll excuse me, I

promised my lovely bride I'd be home by ten." He stands. "I look forward to hearing from you, Ms. Steel."

"It's great to be doing business with you. Have a lovely evening with your wife."

He leaves the table, and I scan the room, hoping to see Rhett, but he's gone. Next up is Luther. I sit patiently and wait for him to use the restroom. I slide out of my seat and stand in the restroom hallway. When he comes out, I trip, falling into him, slipping my hand into his pocket, and pickpocketing his cell phone.

"I'm so sorry," I say.

He smiles. "Don't be. You can bump into me anytime."

My skin crawls from the sleazy look he's giving me. I duck into the bathroom to get away from him and wash my arms where he touched me.

One man brings a tingling sensation to my skin, like when a body part has fallen asleep and comes back to life. The other one sends shivers down my spine and makes me want to vomit.

I exit the restaurant and head straight home to delve into Luther's phone. He's an idiot for keeping his passwords in his Notepad app. As I tap on his phone with one hand, my other Googles the Bond &

Bevel to read about the owner. No picture is attached, but I have a very clear vision of what he looks like, and I can't get him out of my head, nor do I want to. What's he going to think when he finds out who I am, or should I say who I belong to? My heart doesn't care about the age difference. I've never experienced such a deep, instinctive response to a man in my entire life.

The information I gather from Luther's phone is gold. I could easily access his account and wipe out all his money with the click of a button, but what would be the fun in that? Our game is much more enjoyable.

Stripping out of my clothes, I shower, and when I'm done, I wrap a towel snuggly around my breasts, brushing my teeth. A bottle of pills rests just inside my drawer where I keep my toothpaste. I stare at it for a long moment and slam the drawer shut. "I don't need you," I hiss, let my towel drop to the floor, and climb under my silk sheets.

Chapter 6
RHETT

WHAT THE HELL JUST HAPPENED? I felt my soul catch on fire. She's gorgeous. Those steely green round eyes had me sucking air into my lungs and holding my breath for her to speak. Cinnamon stick-colored hair framed her sweet face, and I wanted to run my hands through it. Her skin looked so soft and without blemish other than the cute mole above her lip. Long, lean legs with the perfect amount of curves to her hips. She's sexy even with her blouse buttoned all the way to her neck, but I don't get the feeling she's reserved. She did say she was here on business, and the man she's sitting with is one seriously fortunate man to be in her company.

The last of my Wild Turkey goes down smoothly, and I lick my lips, taking one more glance at her before I vacate my barstool and head toward home. My apartment is within walking distance. The air is warm, but there's a light sea fog rolling in off the water. I hesitate before crossing the street, wanting more than anything to go back inside, take her by the hand, and spend the evening getting to know her.

"A thief." I laugh to myself. She warned me she'd break my heart, but I didn't shy away from the thudding sound my heart made as I watched the words leave her lips.

I lied. I'd be the one breaking her heart. I'd hide who I really am, too flawed to deserve anyone's love. No one would willingly sign up to be in a permanent relationship with me. She would eventually find me too flawed and move on. Everyone has limits.

Tucking my hands deep into my jeans pocket, I shuffle across the street and walk the two blocks to my apartment. It's a building that was built in the 1940s and renovated last year. The lower part has shops. The second story houses adjacent apartments. It's a small space, but it meets my solitary needs. The open area of the living room boasts no furniture. I haven't gotten around to buying any, and I'm not great at decorating. My kitchen, however, has every appliance known to man. I love to cook, and it keeps me busy the times I'm here alone. In the six months I've been here, I've only made one friend.

I've been too busy with the coffee shop and teaching kids the skills of hockey. Ben Steel and I became friends over a cup of specialty coffee I delivered to his chambers. He asked if I'd join him in a day of golf, and unlike me, I accepted, and I'm glad I did.

From day one, I gathered he was a private man like me, and we have a mutual respect for one another. I don't know anything personal about him other than I've heard him mention having daughters.

We play golf, chat about nothing personal, smoke a few cigars, and enjoy a day not filled with a million questions.

My footsteps echo in the room as I enter my bedroom, kick off my shoes, and strip out of my clothes. I switch on the ceiling fan to drown out the voices in my head so that I have a chance of getting a restful night's sleep.

The break of dawn comes too early, and I find myself at the coffee shop before the first employee arrives. My office smells of leather and coffee beans, both of which are things I love. Working with the rawhide keeps my hands busy, and the coffee keeps me alive and sane.

After the morning crew arrives, I make sure they have everything they need before I bolt out the door to the ice rink a mile down the road. A vehicle is something else I haven't had time to buy. I prefer walking. It clears my head.

My gaze swivels like a spinning top and has me nearly toppling over my own feet when I see the gorgeous woman from last night shutting the door on a bright yellow sports car and shrugging her leather bag over her shoulder. The car is fitting because it's as bright as she is. *Perhaps she wasn't lying. A car thief.* I grin at the thought.

I backtrack, holding the door open long before she reaches it. A slow, lazy smile covers her face, and she raises her sunglasses to rest on top of her head, exposing a forehead that I'd like to plant my lips on.

"Hi." A smile toys with the corners of her mouth.

"You came." That statement holds so many meanings.

"You invited me, didn't you?"

At a snail's pace, I rake my gaze over her body. Her emerald-green satiny top is loosely buttoned, but not like last night. The top three are undone, and the soft material lays open, exposing the curve of her breasts along with the edge of her taupe-colored lacy bra. My body involuntarily reacts downright hedonistically. Her white capris follow the curve of her body to her ankles, polished off with a pair of gold sandals. As my gaze shifts upward, I notice her nail color has changed to a bright red, matching her lipstick. I only recall this because when she touched my forehead last night, they were a soft pink. She's gripping a crumbled white bag with the logo from the bakery on Main Street.

"I did." I finally find my voice, and it's sandpaper rough, with my smile mirroring hers.

She walks not only through the door of my business but also through the gaping hole in my heart. She spins to face me. "I stopped at the bakery and brought you something, but I'm afraid there's only crumbs left." She holds the bag between us. "What can I say? I love pumpkin muffins." She lifts one shoulder and scrunches her adorable nose.

My sight locks on the corner of her lip, and I slowly raise my hand, wiping away the crumb on her mouth. "You buy me a muffin and eat it." I grin to keep the longing out of my chest.

"I'm not to be trusted. I did tell you I was a thief." Her head falls back with the most glorious snort.

Is there anything about this woman I don't find sexy? "So you brought me the empty bag to torment me?"

She stares at it. "I couldn't leave the trash in my car. The smell might have me eating the bag itself."

My turn to laugh. I'd love to have been that pumpkin muffin she consumed. "I take it you like food."

"Way more than I should," she snickers.

"It just so happens I love to cook, and I'll have to add pumpkin muffins to our menu."

"I swear the bakery puts an aphrodisiac in their batter." Her hand flies to her hip with lots of sassiness.

"I'll have to get their recipe." I look past her at the clock on the wall, knowing I'm going to be late and catch so much grief from the kids because I drill in them the importance of being on time.

"Am I keeping you from something?" She twists, following my gaze to the clock.

"Regrettably, you caught me leaving."

"And you stayed to see me?"

"Yes," I almost hiss.

She mashes her lips together, rubbing them back and forth.

My jeans feel very constricted at the moment,

and I alleviate some of the stress by rocking back and forth on the heels of my tennis shoes.

"I'm late too. I'll just order a few cups of joe to go." She points to the line at the counter.

"Let me grab them for you before you go. On the house. I'll toss in a few blueberry muffins." I wink and walk behind the counter.

"One caramel latte and one sugar and cinnamon Chai tea," she says.

Two drinks. I wonder who she's meeting.

Thomas bursts through the kitchen door, and his face lights up as if he knows who she is. He greets her with a kiss on her hand, and jealousy hits me like ice cracking on a frozen lake. "Coming right up," I holler.

Her phone pings and she visibly shakes him off to return a text to someone while she waits. Rookie move on Thomas's part. With lips like hers, I'd be seeking them out like a hockey puck going a hundred miles an hour, aiming for its goal.

I peek at the time again. I'm seriously late. The little beasts will make me skate hard and fast for ten minutes like I do them. Perhaps I should reconsider the consequence of tardiness. Before placing the drinks in a cardboard holder and handing them to her, I scribble my phone number on the latte, hoping like mad it's the one she's drinking.

Her green eyes take flight with mine, rocking back and forth. "Where's the muffins," she asks, then her face lights up with a twinkle in her eyes.

I chuckle low in my gut and remove two muffins from the glass counter. "Are you going to share these with whoever you're meeting, or do I need to toss in a couple extra?"

She pats her stomach. "I'm kinda full from pumpkin muffins," she teases.

I walk her to the door and step outside. "Do I get the pleasure of learning your name, or is that second-date material?"

"You consider this a first date?" Her well-manicured brow raises.

"Close enough," I jest.

Her gaze narrows for a moment as if she's sizing me up. "Audrey."

I can't stop my feet from closing the distance between us, letting my breath fall on her tender skin next to her ear. "It's nice to meet you, Audrey."

Goose bumps rise on her neck, and I hear her sharp inhale.

"My name is Rhett Fox," I add, then take a single stride back.

Her steely green eyes have turned more the color of her blouse, and her lips are parted slightly. "Rhett," she rasps.

My name sounds sexy coming from her. "I'll see you soon," I whisper and turn around, walking away but wanting nothing more than to chase her down and hold her captive in my arms.

Picking up my pace, trying to make up the time, I jog the sidewalk. I'm dripping in sweat when I swing open the door to the hockey rink, and the cold air cools me down.

"You're late, Coach Fox." My goalie, Justin Nelson, who we call Nelly, taps his stick on the ice.

"He should have to do laps." The defenseman, Charlie, slaps Nelly on the shoulder pad.

"I agree." Nelly shuts the cage of his helmet.

I'm the coach, and I could fight them on it, but I'll take the hit because these players haven't had good examples in their lives. I consider it my penance for the things I've done. "Alright. Warm up while I get my skates on."

Once I open my locker, it takes me no time at all to suit up and tie my skates. Without hesitation, I speed out on the ice and take hard laps around for ten minutes. I'm panting and drenched again in sweat by the time I dig my blade into the ice, skidding to a stop.

"You're pretty fast for an old man." Filapose high-fives his opposing winger, who they call Lefty.

Santiago and Willie laugh.

"Okay, you've had enough fun at my expense. Get your butts on the ice." I point, and they scatter all except Nelly.

"I bet some hot chick made you late. Unless you're too old for that sort of thing."

"Mind your own business, Nelly." I wave him off. *Too old*. I wouldn't call it old, just lots of experience. I'm betting I'm twenty years or so older than Audrey. He's right. At forty-six, I'm too old for her, but it doesn't stop me from wanting what I can't have.

Folding my arms over my chest, I coach the boys from the sideline, thinking about some of the trouble these boys have been in and their lack of parental guidance. Honestly, they aren't bad kids; they're just misguided. I'm honored to be coaching them, and a few of them have some mad skills. Nelly, if he sticks with it, could go far as a goalie. He needs the support, and that's what I plan on giving him—something I never had from a father.

After two hours of practice, I'm heading back to

the coffee shop to work on a few special-order leather products. I check my phone and sigh. "It was crazy of me to think Audrey would text me." I scratch my soft beard, beating myself up for being attracted to her.

Chapter 7
♥AUDREY

"KNOCK, KNOCK." I tap on Finley's office door and peek inside at the same time.

"Come in," she says, stacking a set of papers together.

"I brought you a latte."

"Thank goodness. I left early for the office and skipped out on coffee this morning. Do I smell blueberry?"

"Yes, courtesy of Rhett Fox," I spit out his name.

"Ah, the two of you finally met."

"You said he was nice on the eyes but you didn't tell me he was akin to a Greek god good-looking." I hand her the cup.

"Please assure me you didn't try to get in his jeans," she huffs. "He's a friend of the judge's, and he's too old for you."

"Is he?" I shut one eye, look up with the other, and press a finger to my bottom lip.

"Don't go borrowing trouble. You'll break his

heart, and Dad will lose a friend. Lord knows he doesn't have enough of those."

"You act like I can't control myself with men." I plop down in a chair.

"You can't. At least not when you're high."

"I bet I can."

"No pills and no sex with Rhett."

"For how long, and what's in it for me?"

She sits and spins in her chair, stopping when she's facing me. "No uppers for six months and sex with the coffee shop owner is off the table indefinitely."

"Wow, you're no fun at all. Why would I ever accept that bet?"

"Okay, no pills ever, and you stay away from Rhett for three months. I figure by then, you'll have moved on with your infatuation with him." She twists a strand of her dark hair between her fingers. "I'll donate a million dollars to your charity if you win."

Leaning forward in the chair, I brace a hand on her desk. "When you lose, you'll sign up for a dating app and choose someone to go out with, and you have to give him three chances before you dump him."

"You're asking a lot." She clucks her tongue.

"When's the last time you've been on a date, if ever?"

"My first year of law school. The judge put an end to it quickly."

"Things are different now."

"How so?" She folds her arms over her chest.

"You're a grown woman, independently wealthy, and capable of deciding for yourself who you want to date."

"Oh really," she snickers. "The judge would put a bullet in any man who'd get close to any of his daughters."

"He hasn't shot Jack yet."

"That's because he knows you're only using him, and you'd never disclose anything to Jack about our family."

Finley is a tightwad, so her giving up a million dollars is huge. Besides, she's probably right. In three months, I'll have no interest in Rhett, so sacrificing him now shouldn't mean anything to me. The drugs will be more difficult. "I'll take your bet." We shake on it.

"Spill the contents of your bag, and I'll expect to sweep your room and vehicle of all pill bottles."

Unzipping my purse, I dump it on her desk, and four bottles roll out, one on the floor.

"Your supplier will be broke," she cracks, sipping her coffee. "Whose phone number is this?" She turns her cup to show me.

"It has to be the barista, Thomas, at Rhett's place. He kisses my hand every time he sees me." I curl my lip.

"Aww, that's so sweet." She laughs.

I memorize the phone number, knowing good and well it belongs to Rhett. What Finley doesn't know won't hurt her. Picking up the cell phone that fell out with the rest of my belongings, I toss it to her. "This belongs to Luther Craig."

"You stole his phone?"

"It was way too easy, and the idiot stores his passwords in his phone. I could bleed him dry without the chase."

"Minus the money in his safe. The judge wants it all."

"You enjoy this as much as he does, don't you?" I narrow my gaze.

"Just like you and James. We all have parts of the game we revel in, but sometimes it doesn't feel like enough."

"I know what you mean." I sigh.

"How about we do this one last job, and the

three of us go to the judge and tell him we're done. It's all of us or nothing."

"It wouldn't take much to persuade James to band together with us."

"No, but she's always the first one to cave in to him when he's angry, just like when we were kids. She couldn't stand the thought of him being mad at her. She said he'd been through enough pain he didn't deserve any more."

"None of us can keep living in the past, including our father."

"Don't count on it. I don't believe he'll ever change."

"According to what you've told me, he did for our mother."

"Yeah, but she was his stabilizer. He's been out of control ever since."

I stand. "We'll finish the job. You talk to James and tell her we're in this together, and she can't back down."

"What am I supposed to do with Luther's phone?" She dangles it delicately between her fingers as if it's contaminated.

I snap it from her. "I'll toss it in the ocean. He might have a tracker on it. I'm headed to my office. I'm going to email you what I've put together regarding the crypto coin. Look it over and add any legalities to it you think it needs."

"I've tons of paperwork to review before my big case on Monday, hence why I'm working the weekend. I won't be able to go over it this week at all."

"Do it when you can. I need time to case out Luther's place. Our old man will just have to be patient."

"Patience and the judge don't play well together," she snickers. "Remember our bet. Stay away from Rhett Fox." She wags a finger.

"Don't worry about me. I have it under control." I'm such a liar even to my own flesh and blood.

As soon as I'm out of the building, I dial the phone number on the cup. It rings a few times, then goes to voicemail. "I should be jealous. You wrote your phone number on my sister's cup, but then again, I call, and you don't answer. I'm sorry you missed me." I hang up, shoving the phone in my purse and digging out my car keys. As I approach my vehicle, I see Jack leaning against the hood.

"Hey, sweetness." He beams from ear to ear.

"What are you doing here? Stalking me?"

"I was in town, and it's hard to miss your car, so I thought I'd wait for you to show up." He places his hands on my hips.

"I told you this wasn't going to happen again between us."

"Yes, but you never mean it. Take one of your pills, and you'll change your mind."

"I've given them up." I push his hands off my hips.

"Since when?"

"About five minutes ago."

"Oh, come on. Don't torment me."

There's a bottle of pills in my glove box. One more time wouldn't hurt, right? "No! I promised Finley I'd steer clear of the uppers."

"For how long?" He scowls.

"Indefinitely." I nod with each syllable.

"If I recall, the last time you swore off drugs, it lasted five hours."

"This time is different."

"So you expect me to walk away from what we have?"

I move past him and unlock the car door. "We have nothing other than sex between us and now that's over."

"You'll change your mind. You're not the type of woman that can go more than three days without sex."

"I have toys. I can use them." I climb into the driver's seat.

"You know where to find me when you change your mind and you run out of batteries."

"I won't." I slam the door. I more than likely will, and it pisses me off. Squealing out of the parking lot, I race onto the highway, shifting into high gear. My phone rings with Rhett's number and connects with my Bluetooth.

I answer, "You're a horrible guesser. The chai was mine."

"I'm grateful it was your sister's cup and not some guy you were meeting up with. Where are you?"

"Speeding down Ocean Drive, waiting for a cop to pull me over any minute."

"You'd look good in handcuffs." His voice is rough and raspy again.

"I prefer pinky fuzzy ones," I jest.

"I'd like to apologize for deserting you this morning."

"What did you have in mind for an apology?"

"Come to my place, and I'll cook dinner for you."

I'll never win the bet if I go to his place. "When and where?"

"I'll text you the address, and now works for me."

"I'll see you soon." I disconnect and wait for his text. "He lives downtown," I mumble and make a U-turn in the middle of the road with horns blaring, but surprisingly, no cop. Weaving in and out of traffic, I get a lot of middle fingers out the window. Taking the off-ramp, I follow the address and parallel park across the street from the Bond & Bevel. Using the crosswalk, I go a block up and see the number on the brick building. The stairs are tucked between two shops and lead to the second floor. I quickly brush my hair with my fingers and dab on a smidge of lip gloss, then knock on his door.

Feet shuffle on what sounds like a wooden floor, and the door opens.

A litany of swear words roll around in my head. For the love of god, he's shirtless and barefoot, with sweat rolling down his temples.

"Audrey," he speaks my name.

Who has a body like that in their forties? He's all hard and toned with six-pack abs and a light dusting of hair in the center of his chest. And how does he smell so damn good?

"Do you want to come inside?" he asks slowly.

"Did…did you not tell me to come right over?" I

bite the corner of my bottom lip and point at his chest.

"I didn't realize you were so close, and I had just gotten home. I thought I'd have time to shower."

"I could leave and come back later when you're fully clothed."

He tugs me inside by the hand. "Don't be silly. Let me go throw a shirt on."

Maybe some shoes too. Even his feet are sexy. He's annoyingly handsome.

Casting my gaze around the room, the place looks like he is in the process of moving in. "You don't have any furniture," I holler.

He comes out of the bedroom, tugging a T-shirt over his head.

"Did you just move in?"

"Six months ago. I don't require much."

"I guess you don't get any company." I laugh.

"You're my first guest."

"Really?" I squint.

"Yes." He chuckles and takes my hand. "Follow me."

We pad across the floor to the kitchen with a long bar in the center. "This is where I spend all my time when I'm home."

I walk around the counter, checking out his appliances. "You don't have a coffee pot?"

"I don't need one. I own the coffee shop," he snickers. "Would you like a glass of wine," he offers.

"Do you have anything stronger?"

He opens a tall cabinet. "Grey Goose, wasn't it?"

"I didn't think you were paying attention at that moment."

"A man would be a fool not to notice you. Do you think I sat on that stool next to you on accident? As soon as I saw you, I wanted to meet you." He takes two glasses from the cabinet and pours our drinks. Then, he removes a metal pan from the fridge and turns on the oven. "I hope you like enchiladas."

"You already have them made?"

"I spend Sundays in the kitchen prepping meals for the week. Otherwise, I'd be eating store-bought frozen meals every night, and I hate those card-board-tasting things."

"Where did you learn how to cook?"

"My grandmother taught me," he says and then grows quiet as if he said more than he wanted to.

"How long were you in the military?"

"I'd rather hear your stories than mine."

"A man of mystery." I walk around to the other side, where he's holding his glass.

"I'm just not big on sharing, that's all."

I can relate to that. "Alright, how about we keep our conversation to the present."

"I like that idea." His smile is back.

"You mentioned hockey. Is that still in the present tense?"

"I pick up a scrimmage game every now and then, but I mostly keep it to coaching."

"I believe you said teen boys."

"Yes. They're a group of kids with troubled pasts, and they are working it out on the ice."

He's got a good heart and a killer body. "Have you ever..." I stop myself before I ask if he's been married. "What other talents do you have?"

"That's a loaded question," he groans, and the sound he makes is so sexy I could orgasm right here and now.

"Your turn. What do you do for a living?"

"I told you, I'm a thief," I roar.

"No, seriously. What is it that you do?"

"I'm an investment broker." He can't say I didn't tell him the truth about both.

"I bet you're really good at it." He smirks.

Taking his glass from him, I lead him over to the window. "See that car." I point.

"Sweet ride. I saw you getting out of it earlier when you stopped by the coffee shop."

"That's how good I am. Do you want to go for a ride?"

"I think you and that car together could be dangerous." His heated stare skims my body.

I playfully swat his cheek. "When you're ready to find out, I'll take you for a spin."

Chapter 8
♥ RHETT

I HAVE to rip my gaze away from her before I crash my mouth to hers. Romantically, I don't fall for women easily, but she makes me want to bare my ugly soul. The things I've done would frighten her, and that's the last thing I want to do. Getting to know her and holding her is at the top of my list. For my own sanity, I sort my life into boxes. Ones I open daily; others are permanently shut, or I'd lose my mind. It's a coping skill I learned in the military after what I had done. The lives I had taken. There's no repentance for me, only forward motion and trying to make other people's lives better.

"I smell. I wouldn't want to stink up your car." I laugh and shove down the emotions that are building in my throat. The heat sensor goes off on the oven, and I place the enchiladas on the middle wire rack.

After a long moment of silence, which seemed more like she was surveying me, she speaks. "You censor yourself."

It's not a question but a statement of fact. "Don't we all?" I ask, tight-lipped.

She angles her head to the side. "I suppose we do."

I walk close to her and skim my fingertip on her lipstick-stained lip. "Are you an open book, Audrey? You did tell me you'd break my heart, but you failed to mention the truth behind it."

"Fair enough," she whispers stiffly.

"But at least you were honest." I drop my hand to my side while her green eyes stay locked on mine, and then she fidgets.

"Honesty isn't always the best policy in my world."

Why do I think she's referring to her personal life as opposed to her work, where I could see to get clients, you'd have to smudge the truth a bit. It's not like I've spilled the truth to her, either. She wouldn't invest time in me if I were honest, but I decide to give an inch.

"My grandmother raised me. She taught me not only how to cook but to bake too."

"The blueberry muffins were her recipe?"

"Yes, and every other Danish you'll find in the coffee shop."

She glances around the kitchen. "You make them here?"

"No. I have a staff that makes them." I reach for the Grey Goose and refill her glass. "Of course, they had to give a blood oath that they wouldn't share the recipe." My face hurts from smiling so wide, and the joke was well worth it when her head falls back in laughter.

"I love your sense of humor."

"I'm only partially kidding." I waggle my brows.

She takes a sip from her drink and that stare is back.

"I already know your next question." I place the bottle on the counter.

"You do, do you?" She smirks.

"You want to know why I was raised by my grandmother."

"The thought had popped into my mind."

"It's a simple answer, but tragic." I gulp down the clear liquid, burning my throat. "My parents were killed in a car crash when I was two years old."

I observe her response for a moment while she tightly grips a locket around her neck, a look of profound comprehension etched on her face.

"I lost my mother when I was two years old also."

I lean back, a single elbow on the counter. "I was so young, I don't remember them, but my grand-mother never stopped talking about them."

"I have two older sisters that were heartbroken but didn't utter her name for years."

"What about your father?"

She lifts her glass in the air. "Now that is what you'd call a loaded question."

Standing tall, I slowly lift my hand to her locket. "What's this? You held onto it when you mentioned your mother."

"It's the only thing I have from her, other than an unread letter." She takes my hand, and places it palm up, laying the still-beating heart in the center of it, then folds my fingers around it.

"Is that a heartbeat?" I frown.

She nods, pursing her lips together. "She had one made for each of us girls before she died, saying we'd always find her here. Of course, I don't remember her actual words, but it's what my sisters told me."

"That's amazing, and what a beautiful gift."

"Sometimes I believe it. When I'm stressed, the heartbeat is stronger and faster, like it's telling me to lean on her."

"She didn't die suddenly." I cradle her cheek in my hand.

"No, it was a long, grueling death by cancer. Her passing changed my father forever." She strolls to the other side of the counter, polishing off her drink, and I notice the faint mist she's fighting off in her eyes.

I know in the depths of my soul, she's just shared something with me that she doesn't ever speak about. Do I push her, asking about the unread letter? No, I need to give her time to breathe. "Thank you for sharing that with me. There are not too many people that I've run into that would understand the grief of losing someone so priceless that you can't recall."

"Enough talk about our pasts. The food smells heavenly." She sniffs the air.

Taking out an oven mitt, I pull down the oven door and look inside. "I'd say we have a ten-minute wait. I'll make a salad to go with it." I shut it and start pulling items out of the fridge.

"How can I help?" she asks, rolling up her sleeves.

"There's a knife over there and a built-in cutting board behind you."

"Toss me what you need chopped," she says, grinning.

While she whittles away at the vegetables, I take down two salad bowls, setting them next to her.

She looks at the bowls and then at me. "You have fine china?"

"They were my grandmother's."

Audrey stops what she's doing and holds my hand. "It sounds like she loved you very much."

I can't hold back when I lower my mouth to hers. The kiss begins gently and sweetly, but when she parts her lips and our tongues intertwine, the desire consumes me with passion. However, I resist the urge and reluctantly disengage, unlocking our lips. "You taste absolutely delicious," I murmur, savoring her lingering essence on my tongue.

"It's the Grey Goose," she razzes.

The timer goes off on the oven, and I reluctantly walk backward, away from her, feeling that momentary connection between the two of us disconnect.

"The salad is ready." She picks up the bowls and sets them in front of two barstools sitting side by side, and it makes me smile.

"I'll plate the enchiladas."

"Do you mind if I fix us some water?"

I point to the cabinet where she can find tall glasses.

"Unless you want something other than water?" she asks, opening the cabinet.

"That's fine."

She takes them down and fills them, using the ice dispenser in the fridge door.

"Investment broker, huh? You wouldn't have any hot tips for a friend?" I sit, tapping the stool next to me for her to sit.

"I don't mix business with pleasure." She half laughs, tossing her long hair over her shoulder.

I'm happy she thinks of me as a pleasure. "I'll remember that next time you want a coffee." I chuckle.

"That's cruel." She holds her hand over her heart.

I can't quit smiling at her. Picking up my fork, I cut off a piece of my enchilada and hold it out for her to taste.

My eyes are drawn to her mouth as she opens it while her gaze is glued to mine. She rakes it off my fork with her teeth, and my cock hardens on demand.

"Hot hot hot!" She sits tall, covering her mouth with her hand. "But so good," she says, slurping a string of cheese between her lips. "I love a man that knows how to cook."

Love, that was my thought exactly, but not about the food. "So, is there something going on with you and my barista, Thomas? Because if there is, I'll have to fire him." I can feel the animation of my own brows.

"Thomas? Oh goodness no. He's handsome and all, but seriously not my type." She drags her napkin into her lap and digs her fork into her food.

"What is your type?"

"Good question. I was literally just asking myself that same thing yesterday." She snaps her mouth around the food. "These enchiladas are wickedly good."

"I love your choice of words," I grunt and subtly shift on my stool to ease the growing discomfort in my jeans.

"I don't think there is such a beast for me. I get bored easily. Men my age are either still searching to find themselves and are selfish, or they don't have a clue."

"What about a man my age?" I ask cautiously.

"They usually have a lot of baggage," she utters between bites. "But I really shouldn't judge people because I have my own fully loaded five-piece luggage set I carry around, zipped up snuggly."

"If you ever care to unload any of it, you know where I live...and work," I add.

"If I told you my deep, dark secrets, I'd have to kill you. Kind of like your secret recipes being exposed."

Our banter flows effortlessly, and I love our dialogues. I could fall into her arms so easily. She's stunning, charismatic, and completely irresistible. It has taken every ounce of my self-control to stay seated near her without giving in to the temptation of running my hands across her body.

When our plates are empty, I pick hers up and take it to the sink. "Would you like something else to drink?"

"No. I'm good. I don't think I can drink or eat another bite." She rubs her stomach.

"No room for dessert then?"

"I'll have to take a rain check." She dabs what's left of her red lipstick from her mouth. "I hate to eat and run, but I really should be going."

As much as I dislike the thought, she should, or she'll be in my bed. "I'll walk you out."

The stairs seem too short of a distance to her car. "This really is a sweet car."

"The offer still stands to take you for a ride."

"How about our next date, I'll let you pick me up." I shrug a shoulder. "Untraditional, I know."

"I'm an unconventional type of woman." Her green eyes are staring at my mouth.

Sweeping a finger under her chin, I lift it slightly and kiss her again. This time, I deepen it, and I can taste her need mingled with mine." Drawing back, I rest my forehead to hers. "Good night, and thank you for letting me apologize."

Chapter 9
♥ AUDREY

I HAD TO LEAVE. There was no other choice, or I would've landed in his bed. It's too bad because he's perfect in every way. He understands secrets, as evidenced by the way he chose his words and what he was willing to share. I understood him and could feel his pain hiding beneath the surface.

Closing the garage door behind me, I have a sole purpose in mind. After discussing our childhood losses, it's time for me to read the letter.

Slipping into my closet, I take down the box containing the envelope and sit cross-legged on the floor. Breaking the seal, I unfold the handwritten final words of my mother while burning the locket into the palm of my hand with my grip.

My dearest sweet baby girl,

· · ·

I'm writing this with a shaky hand because it's not a letter a mother ever wants to write to her daughter. I asked that your father not give you this letter until you were an adult so that I could wish you so many good things in life.

I left you way too early and didn't get a chance to see you grow up, but even at two, I could see who you'd become. Out of our three daughters, you're the most like me, and I know you have my eyes. Eyes that will remind your father of me every day of his life. We'll get to that in a minute, but first I want to talk about you.

You're going to be lost for a while, probably by some misguidance of your father, though I know he means the best for you. Even at two, you were strong and independent, never wanting help with the toughest things you faced. A sense of adventure was bound to be in your future.

When I say you'll get lost, I mean in heart and spirit. You'll know right from wrong, yet war with the sadness inside of you to choose the right path. I know this because you're not only like me, you're your father's child too and when faced with difficulty, he has a tendency to take the road less traveled. My wish for you is to be wild and free but with grace and humility. Be loved and give love with all your heart. Don't let my death have you frozen in time. I gave you my heartbeat, let it guide your path, and know that I will always be with you.

Closing my eyes, I can picture your sweet grown-up face. Green eyes, long locks of brunette hair, and you had the cutest mole above your lip that you used to rub with your tiny fingers. I imagine you hated it growing up as a teenager. It's a beauty mark that you need to flaunt and I wish I was there to tell you how beautiful you are.

I'll miss out on your graduation, watching you fall in love, getting married, and having children, but know I want all those things for you, sweet girl, and if there was any way I could be there, I would. Know that you are loved.

Back to your father, and I'm only writing this to you because I know you'll be the one that owns his rugged heart. He was a man on a path of destruction when I met him. Something drew me to him and wouldn't let me go. I loved him with every ounce of my being. He changed courses for me, and became the man I knew he could be. With me gone, I'm afraid he'll revert back to his old ways because I was his compass in life. As much as I wish he'd stay the man I loved for you girls, I'm afraid he lost his one true north and will change directions again. I need you to love him no matter what. Don't desert him. Coax him back to the light with love and understanding. Be firm, and never be scared to tell him how you feel. It's what he loved most about me.

I'd go on forever in this letter, but I'm so so tired. I LOVE YOU, Audrey Mackenzie Steel. Don't ever forget it and to feel it every time you hold my beating heart.

Your loving mother.
I'll see you again one day.

Tears don't fill my dry eyes like I thought they would, adding more stained splotches to the paper. My heart holds a feeling of peace that she knew me even though I didn't know her. There's a sense of sadness, too, that I'll never have the things she wished for me. Life turned out as she thought it would after she left my father's life. Graduation is the only thing she missed out on with me. I've never fallen in love. Marriage is out of the question, and children are not something I've let myself dream of. How could I? I can't bring them into my world. I fold the letter, tucking it back into place.

Changing out of my clothes, I think about her words. Tonight is the closest I'll ever get to falling in love. My love would only destroy Rhett. I push the notion out of my head and crawl into bed, jonesing for a drug. Instead, I fluff the pillow under my face and stare into the darkness until my eyelids finally give out.

* * *

My dark shades don't allow the morning sun in my bedroom, so when I wake up, I have no idea what time it is, only that it's Sunday. Tugging on a light, silky robe, I head for the coffee pot to find James sitting at the breakfast nook by herself, looking a little green.

"You alright?" I ask, laying my hand gently on her shoulder.

"I need to tell you something I haven't told anyone. Not even Finley."

It's very unusual for her not to tell Finley everything. They've always been so close.

Scooting the wooden chair out, I sit next to her. "I'm listening." I lay my hand on the top of hers resting on the table.

"I'm pregnant." She whispers so softly I'm not sure I heard her correctly.

"What?"

She peers over my shoulder, making sure there is

no one else within earshot. "I'm going to have a baby," she says a little louder.

I can't gauge how she feels over the fear of letting anyone else hear her. "Are you happy about it?"

A slow smile covers her pretty face. "Yes."

"My next obvious question is, who? I didn't think you were messing around with anyone."

"I haven't."

"Well, unless you're the virgin Mary, I don't understand." I squeeze her hand.

"I broke into a sperm bank and stole a vial and had a doctor friend of mine perform an in vitro procedure, and the sperm fertilized my egg."

"Why did you feel the need to steal it? You could have gone through obtaining it legally."

She shrugs. "It would have taken too long."

"I'm happy for you, but what happens now? You have to tell the judge you're pregnant, and his reaction is not going to be one of happiness." I realize how awful this sounds. He should be proud to be a grandfather, but I know the hellfire that's about to rain down on her.

"I'm not going to tell him until I have to. This little one is mine, and I'm keeping it." She places her hand on her flat belly.

"Did Finley get a chance to talk to you yesterday?"

She shakes her head without looking at me.

"This job with Luther is going to be our last one."

Her head whips in my direction. "Really?"

"Yes. I want a normal life. Finley wants one too. And now that you're with child, you deserve one. But you have to be strong. The judge is going to be angry and sad, and you've always given in to his sadness."

"It's different now. I have this little one to think about."

"That's right, you do. So, no matter how badly you feel for him, your life is about this baby."

"What if I'm not enough?" Her head falls downward.

"Look at me," I snap. "You're a grown, intelligent woman with a good profession, and you have two sisters who adore you and will spoil this baby rotten. Don't ever think you aren't good enough because you are."

"Mom used to say those words to me when I'd think I wasn't enough."

"Then I'm glad I could fill her shoes for once. You

and Finley had your hands full trying to raise me when you weren't even grown yourself."

She smiles. "Thank you."

"My advice is tell Finley. We'll put our heads together and inform him not only about the baby but that we are done helping him with his twisted revenge on the world." I stand. "In the meantime, you need to try and eat something."

With the mention of food, she bolts to her feet and out of the room, and I hear her hurling in the bathroom.

"She okay?" Finley points in James's direction as she enters the kitchen.

"Yeah. Just something she ate." I don't want her to hear about the baby from me or that I knew before her.

"How is the setup of Luther going? I couldn't sleep last night, so I looked over the papers you gave me. I added a few things, but all in all, you did good work."

"Seems like none of us sleep well around here," I mumble. "I'll plant the seed with Luther this week. I'm going to invite him to escort me to the gala."

"That should be interesting." She grasps my chin with her hand and draws my face toward hers so she can look into my eyes. "Are you high?"

"Nope, that's why my hand is shaking." I hold it out flat to see the quiver in my fingers.

"And Rhett?" She cocks a brow.

"I haven't seen him." A little white lie falls off my tongue.

She releases me. "I should drug test you, but I'm late, and I'll have to take your word for it."

"You should be practicing your dating skills," I taunt her.

"One thing is for sure. I'll never have to write that check." She wags a finger at me.

"Ye of little faith," I snark, jonesing for a pill.

The judge strolls into the room wearing a pair of khakis and a collared shirt.

"You going to church," I snark, knowing he's not set foot inside a church since Mom died.

"Hardly. I've decided to play a round of golf."

Rhett. "By yourself?"

"No, I'm meeting a friend. I was actually considering having him over for dinner one night so you and James could meet him. Finley met him at my office."

"Here?" I aim a finger at the wood floor. "At our house? You never have people over."

"It's high time I change that." He tucks the tail of his shirt into his khakis.

"That means we can invite people over too?" My voice rises a few surprised octaves.

"Absolutely not." He chuckles.

"So you can have a stranger over to our house, but we can't." My hand lands on my hip.

"That's right. I'm glad we have an understanding." He marches out of the house, hauling his golf clubs over his shoulder.

Rhett cannot come here. He can't know that I'm the judge's daughter.

Shambles leisurely strolls into the room, stops dead in her tracks, and hisses with her spine curled in the air.

I turn to look at what's got her all hot and bothered to see Jack peering into the window.

"What the bloody hell is he doing here," I stammer, swinging open the door. "You can't be here, and you know it! My father is in the garage." I jerk him inside before I hear the lull of the garage door opening.

"I missed you." He tries to put his arms around me.

"Stop!" My hands fly out in front of me, pushing his chest. "I meant what I said. There's no more stopping by whenever you feel like it. No more late-night booty calls. I'm done."

"You don't mean it...unless there is someone else." He drags out the last syllable.

"This has nothing to do with anyone but me. I'm cleaning my act up, and that includes you. I'm sorry. I've used you all these years, and it wasn't fair to you."

"Who are you, and what happened to Audrey?" He scowls.

"I've just come to the harsh realization that I don't want to go through life feeling numb, and that includes you, despite how callous it may sound. I made an effort to be straightforward with you right from the start, although I understand it may not have appeared that way since I was the one maintaining our connection. For that, I genuinely apologize. My intention was never to cause you pain."

He runs a hand through his thick mop of sandy-colored hair, exasperated. "This can't be happening. Take a pill or something." He rips open a drawer, rummaging through it for a bottle.

"I'm asking you nicely to leave."

He wheels around to face me. "How do you expect me to walk out? You're the only woman for me!"

I'd say there were plenty of fish in the sea, but it would only make him angrier.

He snaps his fingers. "You don't think I'm good enough for you. That's why you've kept me a dirty little secret from your old man."

"That's not it at all. That was for your own safety."

"I'm not afraid of the judge." He cocks his shoulders back.

"You should be," I warn.

"I'm not letting you go so easily."

"You don't have a choice, Jack. This is my decision."

His lip curls in a snarl. "You're going to regret it." He wheels around on his feet and storms out, slamming the door so hard the glass in the window rattles.

Chapter 10
♥ AUDREY

BETWEEN TAKING on teaching my coworkers selling skills and working day and night to make sure everything is perfect for setting up Luther, I've hardly had time to breathe. I've made it an entire week without popping a single pill, and I've dang near lost my mind on several tense occasions, mainly in dealing with the judge.

I've stopped by the Bond & Bevel a few times after I watched Rhett exit the building. Avoiding him has only been for his own good. He's texted me several messages, and I've made excuses as to why I can't see him when all I've wanted the entire time is to run to him.

My libido is in overdrive, and I'm not handling it very well because his last text telling me how badly he wanted to kiss me again has me parking my sports car outside the ice rink to watch him coach his team. I can admire Rhett on the bench and not have to be so close to him that I ache.

Buttoning my white denim jacket, I walk

through the doors with a cold blast to the face. Once inside, the rink is filled with spectators. My sight is instantly drawn to Rhett on the other side of the ice, watching his kids skate out to warm up.

As though he has an uncanny ability to detect me, he scans the crowd, and his eyes meet mine before he offers a charming smile. Why does he have to be so incredibly handsome? And dear heavens, he's dressed in a suit. The yearning in my stomach intensifies tenfold. Why, precisely, have I been avoiding him? My father? I could conceal it from him. The million dollars I stand to lose for my charity if I give in? Money is inconsequential. I could recoup that in no time with a few clicks of the keyboard.

To hell with all my justifications. I've never desired a man this intensely, and I'm determined not to maintain this facade any longer. I find a seat next to an older couple in the third row from the bottom.

"That's our grandson." The elderly man speaks loudly with pride in his voice, pointing to one of the kids.

The goalie skates over to Rhett, they chat about something for a moment, and he sends him back on the ice. The other team glides out, and the players are much bigger than Rhett's kids.

The game starts, and I'm on the edge of my seat. The other team may be larger, but The Sharks are much faster and skilled at passing the puck. They seem to play well as a team, while their opponents don't function well together.

Rhett stands, watching and not saying a word. I, on the other hand, am screaming my lungs out. "Are you blind, Ref? He tripped him!" My hands are curved around my mouth. I see Rhett smirking but not looking in my direction.

"You tell him!" the man next to me says.

In the third period, the score is tied at two with one minute left in the game. Our goalie deflects a slap shot, and The Sharks take control, moving the puck down the ice and setting up their play. Our right winger taunts them with a few moves and skates to the right of the goal, then makes a wrist shot from the back of the blade, scoring the final point from a backhanded play. The buzzer sounds, and the players surround one another in a circle, raising their hockey sticks and cheering.

Rhett opens the plexiglass door, rounding them up to go to the locker room. He looks over his shoulder, lifting his chin in the air at me as if asking me to stick around. I acknowledge him with a tilt of my head.

The air is frigid, but my insides are heated up, and it's not from watching the game. Closing my eyes, I can see myself peeling Rhett out of his suit. Make that ripping the buttons off and dragging my teeth down his muscular abs.

"Which one of those kids was yours?" The elderly man nudges me with his elbow, catapulting me out of my delicious fantasy.

"Actually, none of them. I came to support their coach."

"Rhett." The man smiles, and his false teeth shine bright white. "He's been so good for the boys. He's got them on the straight and narrow, and I admire him for not cutting them any slack. You be sure to tell him how proud we are of him."

"I'll do that," I say, even though I didn't catch their names before they gradually make their way up the steps.

I hang out after everyone has left except the cleanup crew. While I wait, I respond to a few client emails. There's a text from the judge wanting to know when I was planning on handing him Luther on a silver platter. I ignore it and scroll to a message from Finley that simply reads one million dollars and stay away from Rhett Fox. I text back the biggest lies I've ever told, "You don't have to worry. I've got things under control."

What is it about this man that seems to have some sort of power over me, and I don't even know him...yet. Other than the fact that he seems to be genuinely good, which normally would have me running full steam in the opposite direction. " A man kisses my hand, and it turns me off," I mumble to myself. But this guy..." If I could see my face, it would remind me of the teenage girl looking dreamily into the mirror, fantasizing about Prince Charming or my knight in shining armor that was going to steal me away from my life. Is Rhett that guy? I mean, I could totally see him playing either role with his killer looks and muscular physique.

Do I need saving? By all appearances, no. I'm fearless, focused, eager, dress and play my part well, and exceedingly intelligent. If you turned me inside out, I'd be splintered, uncertain, haggard, lonely, and some days I don't even want to think an intelligent thought besides shielding myself from my reality, curling into a fetal position, and not moving for days on end.

Wearing my skin right side in as well as the success I've made is what wins out and gets me from day to day. I stifle the rest; albeit through sex and drugs.

"I'm glad you waited for me."

I'm jolted out of my head, hearing Rhett's voice behind me and his footsteps padding down the stairs. I twist, watching him. His suit jacket is over his shoulder, and the muscles in his chest ripple under his fitted shirt with his downward motion. The temperature in the ice rink rises around me, and I tease my lower lip with my teeth.

"Hey," my voice emerges huskily. When he draws nearer, I stand there, taking a moment to admire him.

"Did you enjoy the game?" His fingers toy with a strand of my hair.

"I most certainly did. The boys played a phenomenal game, and their coach looked handsome on the bench."

His grin is shy for the first time. "Thank you." He steps so close I can feel his mouth on the bridge of my ear. "Have you been avoiding me?"

His tone makes my heart feel as if it might burst out of my chest. Instead of choosing a lie, I utter the truth. "Yes."

He takes a step back, snags my hand in his, and full on smiles. "Come on."

"Where are we going?" With excitement, I let him take the lead.

"To my place. But it's not what you think."

"Oh, you mean we're not going to your place so you can strip me out of my clothes?" I laugh but hope I'm wrong, even if it would cost me a million dollars.

He halts on the concrete landing. "As much as I would like that, I have a house guest for the night."

"I take it by the way you worded that, it's not me."

"Nelly's parents are away for the weekend for a business meeting, and they asked if he could stay with me. He tends to keep himself out of trouble when I'm around."

"He's the goalie, right?"

"You were paying attention to the game." He chuckles.

"I love hockey. My father used to drive us to Tampa so my sisters and I could watch the Bolts play once a month."

"Sounds like your father is a good dad."

"He surely loves his girls."

He lays his hands on my hips and pulls me closer. "You take my breath away, and I don't even know your last name."

"Ste...Stephens." I can't tell him. Not yet.

"It's nice to officially meet you, Audrey Stephens. Now come home with me."

My cheeks hurt from smiling. "That sounds like an indecent proposal." I follow him out of the rink, thinking he's leading me to his car.

He shoves his free hand in his pants pocket and keeps his other one on the small of my back as we stroll the sidewalk. "It's a nice evening for a walk," he says, answering the question I didn't ask.

"Do you own a car?"

"There's no need. I live close enough to walk anywhere I need to go, or I call an Uber."

"Well, I do own a vehicle, and I can't leave it parked here, so now is as good of time as any for me to take you for a ride." I tug his hand from my back and twine my fingers with his.

"Alright. Lead the way, but it will be a short ride."

"We could take the long way."

"I'm afraid not. Nelly's parents will be dropping him off shortly, and I kinda need to be there."

"Are you sure you wouldn't rather do this another night?"

"I'm positive. I want to get to know you."

"Did you not heed my warning that I would break your heart," I snicker.

"I did, but I want to know if you're worth the risk." He jerks me to his chest, and his lips land on mine. "You sure taste like you'd be worth it." His words tickle my mouth, and it lights other body parts on fire.

If I give in to my need, we'll be breaking our backs trying to have sex in the small space of my car, and I want space to devour him. "We should go," I rasp, digging into my purse and finding the button to unlock my car.

"You're right." He releases a deep sigh.

He has to fold himself almost in half to get in the passenger seat. Pulling at the seat belt, he fastens it. "I have a feeling I'm going to need this."

I grin and shift into gear. "If we were taking the long way home, I'd insist on you wearing it. Riding through town, there's one too many lights."

"Why do I get the feeling that hasn't stopped you in the past?" His smile is infectious.

It literally takes eight minutes to reach his building. As I parallel park, he points. "They are already here."

He stretches a muscular leg getting out, and I close the driver's side door, locking it. Rhett introduces me to Nelly's parents, and they thank him profusely for helping them out.

Rhett grasps Nelly's shoulder with his large hand. "It's no problem at all." They part with a handshake, and Rhett holds open the door. We take the stairs to his apartment.

"Wow, this place is cool, Coach, but where's the couch?"

He braces his hand on his chin. "Something I haven't gotten around to doing. Perhaps the two of you could help me pick one out."

"I'd be fine with a pillow or two on the floor." Nelly shrugs.

"I think the two of you should let me be in charge of choosing the furniture." I wave a finger between them.

"It sounds like the perfect plan to me. I'll find us something to eat."

"Can we order pizza, Coach?"

"If that's what you want."

"Pepperoni with extra cheese." He plasters on a wide grin, showing his teeth.

"You got it." He angles toward me. "Anything special you'd like on it?"

"I should just let you enjoy his company."

"Please, stay." He traces his finger on my jawline.

"Olives. I love olives on my pizza," I relent.

"I'll call in an order." He digs his phone out of his jacket pocket. "I'm going to go change into something more comfortable while I place our order."

What I wouldn't give to watch him take off his clothes and see him bare. It would be a thing of beauty. Instead, I move to where Nelly has made himself comfortable on one of the stools at the breakfast bar, and he's setting up a laptop he removed from his bag.

"You played really well tonight."

"Thanks to Coach's advice." He taps the keys.

A kid his age, I would think he'd be pulling up a game or music. I'm surprised when he Googles furniture. "I thought you were going to leave the furniture buying to me?"

"The man needs some serious help." He shakes his head. "He can't have a beautiful woman over in an empty apartment."

"You're right. We need a place to curl up and watch movies." I scoot my chair closer to his and look at the photos of couches.

"For that to happen, he'd have to have a television." He rolls his eyes.

"True." I curl my lip. "Which one do you like?"

His eyes grow wide when he clicks on the prices. "No wonder his living room is empty."

"I like this one." I touch the screen, showing him a camel-colored leather couch.

"He makes that kind of money being a coach?"

"He's not only a coach. He owns the coffee house down the road."

"I don't know. Stealing what you want seems a lot easier."

"You've been in a bit of trouble, haven't you?"

"Yeah. I got caught red-handed stuffing a video game in my backpack." He twists his mouth to the side.

"Taking something that isn't yours is wrong."

"Is stealing ever right?" He looks up at me.

I'm the last person he should be asking. "In some instances..." I'm cut off when Rhett comes into the kitchen wearing a pair of jeans and a loose-fitting T-shirt with no shoes on his feet.

"Stealing is never right." He frowns at me.

I straighten my spine. "What if he was hungry and had no food, and the only way he could get it was by taking it?"

"Then you ask for help or go to a food bank."

"What if someone stole something priceless

from you, and you returned the favor?" I'm feeling him out.

"Stealing is wrong no matter how you look at it," he almost growls.

And there's my answer. Not only will I break his heart, he'll shatter mine.

Rhett comes around to face the screen. "Is that the one you like?" He points.

I nod, flattening my lips together.

He digs a credit card from his wallet. "Order it."

Nelly takes it from him. "This is so cool. I've never used a credit card before." He enters the information.

Rhett works on taking down plates and glasses. I stare at his backside, longing for something I can't have.

They talk about the game and strategize for the next one. I enjoy listening to them banter back and forth. This is the life Rhett's meant for, not getting involved with someone like me.

The pizza arrives, and as soon as the square box hits the table, Nelly dives right in, taking a huge bite with a piece of cheese dangling from his chin. Once we're done, I sling my purse over my shoulder. "I really should get going."

Nelly's gaze bounces between the two of us. "I'm sorry I cramped your style."

Rhett ruffles the kid's hair. "You didn't."

"He's right. I'm the one that busted up your evening. It was very nice to meet you," I tell him.

"Will I see you at my next game?"

I don't want to lie to him. "I'll check my schedule."

"I'll walk you out," Rhett says. "You stay out of trouble," he tells Nelly.

"This place is empty. How much trouble could I possibly get into?" He laughs.

"You've got a point. I'll be right back."

"If I were you walking a pretty girl out, I'd sure take my time," he hollers before the door closes behind us.

"Smart kid." He chuckles, holding the door open to the outside.

"Thank you for the pizza."

"We should do this another time without the kid here." He draws me into him.

"I had a nice time tonight." I don't verbalize the "but we shouldn't be together, and it will never work" part. He kisses me and I cry on the inside. When our mouths part, he's as heated as I am.

"Good night," he rasps with his forehead glued to mine.

I free myself from him. "Night."

He opens the door for me and slowly shuts it. Pressing the button to start my car, I wait for him to move to the sidewalk until I veer onto the street. Without thinking, I open the console, searching for a pill bottle, only to come up empty-handed. Switching on my Bluetooth, I call my dealer, placing an order not only for me but also for what I'll need for Luther.

Chapter 11
♥ RHETT

"DAMN, SHE'S BEAUTIFUL." The hot evening breeze does nothing to cool me down. I reluctantly watch her drive off. "She showed up," I whisper to myself. I was drawn to her the moment she walked into the ice rink. It was hard to stay focused on the boys when all I wanted to do was be near her. My heart squeezed when I heard her cheering on the team and all but cursing out the refs for bad calls. This woman has gotten under my skin. The question is, could she live with the things I've done?

Swinging the glass door open, I stride into my apartment, finding Nelly right where I left him with his earbuds firmly in place. Audrey was so good with him until she tried to justify any reason to steal. I'm not in disagreement with her about situations when I could see the person's reasonings, but for him, I had to remain firm. She was even gorgeous when a ghost of a smile played across her face when I cut her off.

I tap Nelly on the shoulder, and he tugs his left earbud out. "You take the bed. I'll make a pallet on the floor. But you need to shower before you get under the sheets. You smell, man." I scrunch my nose in exaggeration.

He sniffs his pits. "I've smelt worse."

"The shower's not an option." I quirk a brow.

"Fine." He closes his laptop.

"Good man," I say, and he hops off the stool.

"You'll find everything you need already in the bathroom."

"Why would you choose to have me stay the night over her?"

"We're friends. That's all."

"I'm a kid, and even I can see the way you look at her. She is definitely not in the friend zone." His gaze finds the ceiling again as he disappears into the bedroom.

"If it were only that simple, kid," I groan.

Monday comes around quickly. After Nelly's parents picked him up this morning, I strolled to the coffee shop that was already bursting with customers.

Stilling myself in my office, I work on a specialty order for a carry-on piece of luggage.

Thomas pokes his head inside. "An order came in for Judge Steel. Do you want me to run it over to him?"

"No. I could use the break. I'll do it."

He lets me know when it's ready, and I carry the coffee to the courthouse. Once I'm let through the security sensors, I take the elevator to his office. His secretary smiles and waves me to his door.

"Knock, knock," I say, inching inside.

"Hey, I was hoping you'd deliver." He gets up from his leather chair and greets me with a handshake. "I see you brought two. Do you have time to join me?"

"I'll make the time." We move to the sitting area of his office.

"We need to set a tee time for Friday." He takes the lid off his sturdy paper cup and blows on the coffee.

"Does one o'clock work for you?"

"I'll have my secretary clear my schedule."

"Consider it scheduled." I join him in cooling off my drink.

"There's a charity gala this weekend. You should attend."

I brace my arm on the back of the couch and cross an ankle over a knee. "What's the charity for?"

"Raising money for cancer victims and their families."

"Sounds like a good cause. Count me in."

He exhales a long breath. "It's one near and dear to my heart."

Ben has never disclosed anything personal about himself other than I've heard him mention his daughters and even that was vague. I've met Finley, but the other two remain a mystery. "How so?"

"My wife died of cancer many years ago."

I drop my foot to the floor. "I'm so sorry."

He waves me off. "As I said, it was a long time ago." His words aren't harsh, but there's bitterness behind his eyes, and the wrinkles deepen.

"I'll happily donate to the charity."

"It's a big deal in this town. Suits, ties, ladies wear long gowns, the whole shebang."

"Will your daughters be attending?"

His gaze skates to mine. "Yes." His tone is almost a hiss of a warning. "My youngest daughter, Audey, doesn't like to make it known, but it's her baby."

"In honor of her mother," I add.

"I'm very proud of the work she's done in raising the money for families in need."

"I'm sure you are."

He rests back in the high-winged chair. "We've never discussed this, but my daughters are all smart, beautiful, successful women, and I'm very protective of them and particular about the men in their lives." He scoots forward in his seat. "Am I making myself clear?"

I laugh. "Abundantly."

He rolls his tongue over his teeth. "You aren't married," he points out.

"No. Never have been."

"We're friends, but my girls are off-limits even to you."

"Don't worry. I have someone that I'm interested in already."

That seems to ease his worry. "Good because I enjoy playing golf with you, and I'd hate to give up the best coffee in town." He smiles without showing his teeth.

"I certainly don't want that." I chuckle.

"Who is this woman that's caught your eye?"

I lean forward, running my hand over my face. "She's amazing, but I'm just getting to know her. So far, there isn't anything I don't like about her. I'd like to take it slow because I get the feeling she's gun-shy about commitment."

"If you'll allow me to give you a piece of advice."

"I'm listening."

"If you find a woman that captures your soul, don't waste time because none of us are promised tomorrow." I open my mouth to speak, and he lifts his hand to stop me. "Before you say anything else, I know what went down in Afghanistan."

My brow furrows. "What?"

"It's ingrained in me to be cautious of the people I surround myself with, which I can count on one hand." He holds up a single digit. "I've read the reports. You're the kind of man who lives with guilt, and I know this because you spend your spare time with those boys on your hockey team."

I stand and pace. "I haven't shared what happened to anyone other than my assigned military therapist."

"You don't have to worry about me telling anyone. I'm good at keeping secrets, but I'm also a man who lives with deep-seated guilt."

I stop and stare at him.

"I'm telling you this so you'll let yourself off the hook. From what I've read, it wasn't your fault. Being that you've never been married or, as far as I can tell, in any committed relationship, I assume you let your guilt get in the way. Don't. If you get the chance to love a good woman, take it."

I ease down onto the couch again. "Your wife must have loved you very much."

"She was the best thing that ever happened to my sorry ass, and her death was the worst day of my life. I'll never have that type of love again."

I reach over and touch his forearm. "You were a lucky man to have it once. I'll keep your advice in mind."

"Good." He stands. "I'll see you on the golf course Friday at one."

"Text me the details of the gala."

"I will."

Chapter 12
♥ AUDREY

"HEY, what are you doing up so early?" I tie my robe as I walk into the kitchen.

"I could ask the same thing of you." James is wringing her hands together in her lap.

"You okay?" I gently touch her shoulder.

"I'm going to tell him I'm pregnant."

"The judge?" I slide the chair out next to her, taking a seat.

"Yes. He's going to find out sooner or later, and I'd rather get it over with."

"Then I'll hold your hand while you do it."

"What's going on in here?" Finley adjusts her bun, then runs her hands down her suit.

"James is going to tell our father the good news."

Finley lifts her wrist to see the time. "Let me make a call to cancel my meeting. We'll tell him together." She skates out of the room with her phone pressed to her ear.

"Have you been able to keep anything down? You look kind of green."

"Yesterday was rough, but I've sipped on some water this morning."

"You've always liked ginger ale when you've had an upset stomach. I'll run to the store and pick up a couple of two-liter bottles."

"No. Thank you, but I have to be at work at noon today. I'll get some on my way to the hospital."

"Maybe you should take a few days off until you're feeling better."

"Okay, I'm here for you now." Finley pops back into the room and joins us at the table.

"Thank you," James says, licking her dry lips.

"Well, all three of my girls at once, and there's no family meeting." The judge adjusts his tie and tucks in the tail of his shirt.

"We're calling a family meeting," I say boldly. "Sit down. We need to talk to you."

"I'm due in court in an hour. Can it wait?"

"No," Finley snaps sharply.

"Are you three planning a coup? I don't have time to deal with this right now."

"Dad, please sit," James finds her voice. "I have something I need to tell you."

"Alright." He sighs loudly, sitting directly across from us. "What is it?" He lays his arms on the table from the elbows down with his palms flat.

"I'm pregnant," she states flatly.

He laughs. "No, really, what is it you want to discuss?"

"She's serious." Finley crosses her arms over her chest.

All the blood drains from his face, and you can feel his anger vibrating the table. His stare bores into James like a palpable flame. "Who the hell is the father?" His teeth gnash, and his lip curls.

"That's not important. She's having a baby." I drape my arm protectively around James.

"Like hell it isn't!" he snarls and nearly flips the table over when he jumps to his feet. "Have I not made myself clear all these years that we can't let anyone inside of this family! I'll kill whoever it is before I'll let him take us down!"

A shiver bolts down my spine. I've never seen him so angry. "You'd murder the father of her baby?" My voice rises. My mind races. *Has he killed someone before?*

"You'll get rid of it so I don't have to," he spats.

James's entire body shakes when she stands. "I'll do no such thing. There is no father, so you don't have to worry about it."

He jerks his head backward. "What do you mean?"

"She used a sperm donor." Finley reaches and holds James's hand.

His shoulders relax, and his head falls back. "Why didn't you start with that?"

"You are unbelievable. We've all sacrificed our lives for your cause, and you'd really kill someone we love to keep your secrets!" My chair falls over as I scramble to my feet. "Luther Craig is the last time we'll steal for you!"

"You think this is all just for me? You girls enjoy taking people down as much as I do. It's for the memory of your mother!" His face grows red.

I clasp the locket. "She would hate this! I can feel it."

"All you can feel is the heartbeat she recorded."

"No. It speeds up when things aren't right and slows to a gallop when things are peaceful."

"That's impossible!"

James and Finley clutch their lockets and then hold mine. They both gasp. "I feel it," they say in unison.

"Mine doesn't do that," James says.

"Mine either," Finley's eyes are wide.

"You girls believe what you want, but this conversation is not over. You're not allowed to quit on this family!" He storms out of the room.

"That went well," James speaks softly. "He's not happy for me at all."

"Once he cools down, he will be," Finley reassures her.

"I can't stay here. I won't have my child living the way we have all these years carrying out his vendetta."

For the first time in my life, I'm truly afraid of our father. If she leaves, will he hunt her down? "We'll find a way for you and this baby to be on your own, out of his reach."

Finley paces the floor. "I watch him and even admire him daily, sitting in the courtroom. He hands down sentences without blinking an eye as if they were candy. How does he do it and not feel one ounce of guilt for the crimes he commits?"

"He justifies it like we all have. We steal from the bad guys and give it to those who deserve it. He's instilled in us a 'Robin Hood' complex, and we've been perfectly happy wreaking havoc on whomever he deems guilty."

Shambles jumps on the table, rubbing her head on my elbow. I pick her up, thinking she's the only thing that loves me outside of this family.

"I don't think I can look at him the same on that pulpit banging his gavel."

My mother's written words ring loudly in my head. *I need you to love him no matter what. Don't desert him.* "We'll figure this out. I'll talk some sense into him."

Finley's hand lands on my shoulder. "If anyone has ever been able to rein him in, it's you. Good luck." She hugs James and hustles out the door.

James's eyes fill with tears.

"Look at me. This baby is going to be loved and will have a normal life. I promise."

"How?"

"I don't have the answer yet, but I'm not going to let him hold you captive for his ideals any longer. Go wipe your face and put your fake smile on. You've got lives to save."

She wipes her nose with the back of her hand. "You sound like someone's mom."

"I'll never have that title, but you will." I lay my hand on her stomach.

"Thank you for being here with me."

"You're welcome."

"Where are we with Luther and his safe?"

"I'm laying the groundwork today. By next week, we should be breaking into his safe, and this will all be over soon." I kiss her cheek and set Shambles on the floor. She protests loudly. "Sorry, baby, I've got to get to work. Go sleep in my bed or do whatever cats do all day long when their owners aren't home." Her long tail flounces in the air as she struts off like a queen.

I hustle to get to the office to find Colin looking through my files. "Can I help you with something?"

He jumps and throws his shoulders back. "I didn't know you were coming in today."

"What are you doing snooping around in my office?"

"I wasn't snooping. I was assessing what you've been investing in lately."

"I send you monthly reports on my clients."

"You never told me how it went with Daryl Brown."

"I got him on board."

"Damn, you're good."

"I still don't understand what you are doing in my office."

"You've been researching crypto coins."

I stare at him with no response.

"I want in on whatever it is you're investing in."

"I'm not. And you went through my search history?" My voice rises.

"Come on." He struts within a few feet of me. "I need a good investment that the team can share with their clients."

"I was doing research for a client. I have no intention of investing in a coin."

"Then give me something I can share with them. I need someone besides you making this firm money."

Walking over to my computer, I pull up a file and email it to him. "Don't say I'm not a team player. Now, get out of my office. I have work to do."

"It's been good seeing you around here more."

"Don't get used to it. I much prefer being beachside."

He raps the doorframe with his knuckles when he finally leaves.

I tap into my private, securely locked files and print the paperwork Finley worked on for the coin to con Luther into buying it. This time, I make sure to go back and erase my history for all of my searches.

My phone pings with a message from Rhett.

I've been thinking about you all day. Come by later and I'll buy you a coffee.

. . .

I want to scream yes, but I can't, especially after the way my father reacted this morning with James.

Sorry. I'm working late. Another time.

It's almost seven when I lock up the office behind me and drive to The Meat Market Steakhouse, where I know I'll find Luther. I smack on some lip gloss, tousle my hair, and unfasten the top three buttons on my blouse, exposing the white lace of my bra. "That should get his attention." Before I hand over my keys to the valet, I change out of my shoes to a pair of four-inch red heels, and sway inside the restaurant.

Luther is seated three barstools down from where he was before, and the seat next to him is empty. I casually make my way toward him, pushing my sunglasses on top of my head. "Is this seat taken?" I ask with a plastered-on smile.

"It is now." He grins. "Do I know you from somewhere?" His gaze takes a leisurely stroll down my legs.

"I don't believe we've met before."

"It will come to me." He taps his chin with his pointer finger.

"Vodka on the rocks," I tell the bartender when he looks in my direction.

"I got it!" Luther snaps his fingers. "I ran into you by the restroom the same night I lost my phone."

"Ah, that's right," I play along. "Sorry to hear about your phone. Did you ever find it?"

"It was the weirdest thing. I have a tracker on it, but I was never able to locate it. My name is Luther." He extends his hand.

"That's too bad. I know how important a phone can be for business. What did you say you do for a living? Audrey." I go to shake it, and he twists my hand over and holds my hand in both of his.

"I sell insurance. What does a pretty woman like you do? Are you a model?"

"Hardly. I'm an investment broker." *Asshat pickup line.*

If someone's ears could literally perk up, his do. "Really. I'd love some investment advice."

He's making this too easy, but I want to string him along so I can gain access to his house. "I'm sorry, I don't give away free advice. If I did, I'd be broke." The bartender sets my drink in front of me.

"Fair enough. How about I buy you a meal, and we can get to know one another."

"I'd like that." I feel acid burning in my throat. This would be so much simpler if I dropped a couple of the pills I bought from my dealer in his drink. The thought of spending time with him repulses me.

"I'll get us a table." He stands.

"I'm fine to eat at the bar if you are." I don't want a table for two.

"Alright." He sits back down and asks for a menu.

"Tell me about yourself other than the fact that you're an insurance agent." I smile and gaze into his eyes like I'm interested. The only thing I want to know is who is the better liar. Me or him?

"I'm single." He holds up his hand so that I can see he's not wearing a ring. "Never been married."

Lie number one.

"So, no kids."

"No."

A man who lies about not having kids is lower than the belly of a snake.

"What do you do for fun?"

"I love a good blackjack table."

One truth, two lies. "Do you play at the Hard Rock in Tampa?"

"I have, but I much prefer Vegas."

Two to two. "Are you any good at it?"

"I'd say so. I made enough money last year to pay cash for a brand-new BMW."

Using other people's money. "Nice."

"In fact, I've held enough cash back that I could invest in whatever you recommend."

I click my tongue. "I do have an up-and-coming crypto coin I've been doing a lot of research on, and I think it could be a good investment for a man like you who is willing to gamble for a good return."

"Let's order our food, and you can tell me all about it."

He lays his hand on my thigh, and I want to grab the steak knife off the table within reach of me and stab him with it. "Alright." I smile, grabbing the menu.

We order, and he periodically touches me as he makes conversation that I couldn't care less about, but I have my fake words and smile locked down enough that he thinks I'm interested in him.

He's mid-conversation, blabbing about something, when I see Jack stalking in my direction. I grind my teeth, preparing for battle. He's going to screw things up.

"I see you moved on pretty quickly." His wide jaw clenches, and his blue eyes are filled with jealousy.

Luther's penny loafers hit the ground, and he stretches to be as tall as Jack. "Is there a problem?"

"You could say so. She's my woman."

"Oh, good grief, Jack. I don't belong to you or anyone else."

"I think you should leave." Luther throws his shoulders back.

Jack stands nose to nose with him. "And you think you're going to make me," he hisses.

I get up and push between them, facing Jack. "Please don't do this."

"Then leave this jerk and come home with me where you belong."

"I don't belong to you, Jack. You have to accept it."

He spins in a circle and comes back with his fist in the air, planting it into Luther's jaw.

"Jack!" I scream when Luther falls back against the bar and then hits the ground.

In any other circumstance, I'd be cheering Jack on for hitting the asshole in the face, but he's ruining my plan.

People scramble around us, and the manager comes over, hauling Jack out of the restaurant.

"Are you okay?" I ask, hoping he's missing a few teeth as I help him off the floor.

"Someone's not too happy you dumped him." He rubs his jaw.

"I'm so sorry." I run my hand down his sleeve.

"I've lost my appetite, and I don't need drama in my life." He tosses cash on the bar.

He means he doesn't need trouble, which seems to follow him. "Let me make it up to you."

"How do you propose to do that?"

"There's a gala Saturday night. Be my date, and I'll make sure you're the first one in on the investment before it's released to the public."

"I like the sound of that." He rocks his jaw back and forth.

I take a pen from my purse, write down the address to the gala on a bar napkin, and stuff it in his pocket. "Meet me there at seven sharp."

"I usually pick up my dates."

"I'll be in meetings all day. I'll change at the office, so it's best if I meet you there."

He steps up close to me. "You're not only beautiful but smart as well. A woman like you will make it financially worth my while, and we can connect on another level."

My pen is still clutched in my fist, and I could easily stab it into his eye. "I'd like that." That comment makes me the biggest liar. I win the gold medal of lies tonight.

Chapter 13
♥ AUDREY

I COVER my hair when a light mist of rain starts to fall. The weather channel has predicted a down-pour and strong winds to kick up sometime late in the evening. I'm thankful the gala is inside this year, being held at the members-only private country club. The judge's clout and a hefty amount of money opened up the doors for the gala to be open to outsiders by invitation only.

My silky forest green dress swishes at my ankles when I walk delicately on the black silhouettes I purchased on my trip to Italy last year when I jetted off to meet a potential investor who I had eating out of the palm of my hands within twenty minutes of meeting her. It was my first encounter with a female client. I honestly enjoyed meeting her, and we had a lot in common. In another life, she and I could have been best friends.

A wisp of my hair falls, framing my face when I reach the entryway. I flash them my ID.

"No need, Ms. Steel. I know who you are." He smiles, holding open the doors.

"I have a guest who will be joining me. Give him my invitation, please." I hand it to him, and he reads the name on the card. "Luther Craig. I'll be sure to let him in for you. Have a good evening."

"Thank you." Once I'm inside, I remove my shawl, handing it to the man handling the coat closet. The country club is decorated just as I instructed with big crystal chandeliers and candles with bright pink flowers on every table. Nestled in the middle is a large open dance floor, a stage on the far side for the classical band, and an open mic for the MC I hired under the foundation's name.

"You look exceedingly elegant," the judge says, moving toward me with Finley on his elbow. She's wearing a burnt orange-colored dress that hugs her curves, and she's left her long hair down with the ends curled.

"Weren't you Finley's date to the prom?" I tease.

"As a matter of fact, I was." He greets me with a kiss.

"Where is James?" I direct my question to my oldest sister because the last time I spoke with James, she wasn't speaking to our father. I can't say that I blame her one bit.

"She got called in on an emergency. She's hoping to make it before the gala is over."

"She's still mad at me." He sighs.

"You were an ass to her, so what do you expect?"

"That's one thing I love about you, Audrey, it's that you aren't afraid to speak your mind." He kisses my cheek.

"If you'll excuse me, I'm going to hit the champagne fountain."

"I'll join you." Finley drops her hand from his elbow and attaches it to mine. "James told me you invited Luther to be your plus one," she whispers.

"I didn't have a choice after Jack punched him in the face. I mean, inwardly, I was cheering him on, but he ruined my game plan."

"This should be interesting, to say the least."

"If it were any other man, the judge would lose his mind. He'll play along, knowing it's part of the game. At least Jack wasn't invited to the party."

"So what is the game plan?"

"I'm going to pop a few pills in his drink when he takes me back to his place. Then James and I can crack his safe, and he'll be none the wiser."

"I thought I confiscated all of your drugs."

"These were bought with Luther in mind."

She jerks my chin toward her. "You aren't high, are you?"

"As much as I'd like to be, no."

"And you haven't slept with Rhett?"

"You were right. I've already lost interest. I'm not good enough for him anyway." The first part is most certainly a lie; the second is the truth.

"I knew it wouldn't take you long."

"Looks like you'll be writing a big fat check."

"I'm proud of you and this foundation. It's helped an enormous amount of families who wouldn't otherwise be able to get the treatments they need. More importantly, Mom would be proud of you."

I involuntarily touch my locket, feeling her heart at ease. "I hope so. Perhaps it would make up for all the other things I've done."

"You know how much that has given back too."

"I don't think outsiders would consider thieves like us something to be proud of."

"Thanks for leaving the invitation at the door."

I spin around to see Luther, dressed in a gray suit with a dark navy shirt beneath his jacket. He's clean-shaven, and his boyish charm shows in his dimples.

"You look nice." My mask of a smile is in place.

"And you look like a princess."

"This is my sister, Finley."

"It's very nice to meet you. Beauty runs in your family."

He's such a smooth talker it makes me want to gag. "Would you like a drink?" I hold up a flute of champagne.

"I think I'll hit the open bar I saw when I was ushered inside."

"I'll wait right here for you."

"Gag a maggot," Finley says from the corner of her mouth when he walks away. "Do women really fall for that crap?"

"They say there's someone for everyone." I shrug and look around the room that's filling up with guests. "It should be a good night for the gala. There is lots of money walking through the doors."

"Well, you and our father did handpick the guests."

I gasp and almost drop my champagne when Rhett walks through the doors wearing a black tuxedo. "Who invited him?"

Finley glances around until she sees him. "Our father."

"He can't see me." I duck behind her.

"Why not?"

"He doesn't know I'm the judge's daughter."

"You didn't tell him?" she scoffs.

"No."

She turns around to look at me. "You lied. You are still interested in him." She aims a long French manicured nail at me.

"I only partially lied. I haven't slept with him." I peek around her. "Why does he have to be so damn sexy?"

"This is not going to bode well for you."

"No kidding. I have to keep him away from Luther."

"Forget Luther. If Dad finds out you like Rhett, he'll snap him in two."

"You have to run interference for me. Keep the three of them away from one another."

"I don't know how you expect me to do that when our father invited Rhett."

My head starts to spin, and I squeeze my eyes shut. "This can't be happening. This is not how I wanted Rhett to find out I'm a Steel. I lied about my last name, for god's sake."

"I'll keep Rhett away from Luther, but keeping him away from the judge will be asking the impossible. It will be my pleasure to keep Rhett entertained," she purrs.

I swat her in the arm. "Don't go entertaining him too much."

She scowls. "You really like him, don't you?"

"Does it really matter? Because if he finds out I'm a thief, he'll turn his back on me."

"You don't know that for sure."

"Trust me, I do." I give her a little shove to go to him.

"I take it by the setup, there will be dancing." Luther meanders back over to me with one hand casually in his pants pocket and the other one holding a martini.

"How about I show you around the country club." My hand goes to his arm, and I escort him in the opposite direction from Rhett and run smack dab into my father.

"I see you have a date tonight." His tone is solid as he introduces himself to Luther, who shakes his hand firmly.

"It's a pleasure to be escorting your beautiful daughter to such an elegant event, Mr. Steel."

"Judge Steel," my father purposely clarifies.

Luther's Adam's apple bobs when he swallows hard, giving away his nervousness at his title. "Judge."

"I'll leave you two alone to enjoy the evening." My father tweaks my arm when he passes by me.

"You didn't tell me your father is a judge."

"Does it matter? You want investment advice. My father has nothing to do with it."

"Are you going to share the recommendation you spoke about to me?"

"I don't think tonight is an appropriate time to get into a deep discussion about it. Give me your email, and I'll send you the prospect on it. We can set up another time to meet."

"A second date." His cheesy smile is nauseating.

"I'd like that very much." I want to rip my own lips off when I brush my mouth to his. He tries to deepen the kiss, but I pull away. "I need another drink. Would you mind refilling it for me?" I bat my lashes.

"Anything for you." He blows me a kiss as he walks away.

"I loathe him," I grit between my teeth, and I can't wait for this job to be over.

"That dress is the perfect color on you." I hear Rhett's voice coming from behind me.

I slowly pivot to face him. "I wasn't expecting to see you here tonight. You look handsome in your tux."

"I didn't know you were on the guest list either." His appreciative gaze warms my insides. "A friend of mine invited me, and right now, looking at you, I'm very glad that he did." He trails his fingertips down my bare arm, and I pray my father isn't watching. I sound like a teenage girl rather than the grown woman that I am. The grown woman in me wants to lead him into the coat room and have my way with him. "I heard the music start playing before I saw you. Would you like to dance?"

Yes, yes, and yes. "I'm afraid I can't." I see Luther headed straight for me, and Finley is nowhere in sight.

"Why not?" He frowns.

"Because I have a date." Luther steps up beside me, handing me a flute of champagne, which, right now, I wish was the entire fountain.

"A date." He steps back, taking in Luther.

"Her dance card is full," Luther snaps, then twists his chin in my direction. "We aren't going to have a repeat of the other night, are we? How many exes do you have?"

"What the hell is he talking about?" Rhett all but growls.

"It's not what you think. It's business."

"His hand on the small of your back doesn't look

much like business to me," he snarls.

"It's not." Luther can't keep his big mouth shut.

A hand lands on my shoulder. "I see you finally met my youngest daughter."

This night couldn't get any worse. Just shoot me now.

Rhett's mouth falls open. He looks at me, then at my father, then back at me. "You said your last name was Stephens," he murmurs.

The look on his face shreds my cold heart. "I—"

"I have a few people I'd like to introduce you to." My father drags Rhett away, and I watch him glance back at me over his shoulder in shock.

"How about that dance?" Luther is grating on my last nerve, and the thought of his hands touching me is absolutely unbearable. "We have to sign up as a couple to enter the dance. It's set up as a dance contest. They can eliminate one or both of us."

"I'm a good dancer." He grins, snagging my hand.

"I highly doubt it," I mumble under my breath. I spent years in dance lessons because my father insisted on his girls knowing how to dance and mingle with rich people.

Thankfully, the music has stopped, and the MC

has taken over the microphone, announcing goals for the evening. He displays a screen with the numbers that have already been raised this year with a long list of families who've received the donations. My charity doesn't keep one red cent. I pay the few employees I have out of my own pocket under a fake corporation name, so they can't pin it back to me.

"I'd love for you all to be able to thank the person who runs the charity, but as you know, the name is anonymous. But I'd like to think the person is in this room tonight, so let's give him or her a round of applause for their generosity."

The room fills with guests clapping. I fill with pride, knowing my mother is smiling down on me in this moment.

"Food will be served shortly, and make sure to pull out your wallets while you see children's faces fill the screen. Each one of them needs your help."

I cringe when I realize our family is assigned to a table together, which means Rhett will be sitting with us. "This is our table." I lead Luther over to it, and he pulls out my chair for me.

The corners of Finley's mouth turn down with her shrug when she sits next to me.

"Sorry, I'm late. What did I miss?" James says,

scooping her long teal dress beneath her when she sits.

"A lot," Finley voices, gulping down her champagne.

Rhett's jaw flexes, and I can tell he's gnawing on the inside of his cheek when he and the judge sit diagonally from us.

I suck in a breath when Luther's hand finds my knee under the table. *Don't kill him. Don't kill him*, becomes my mantra. I have to play the part. The glare in Rhett's eye says he hates me, so I have nothing else to lose. I lean over and kiss Luther on the cheek, and he tightens his grip on my knee.

"If you'll excuse me." Rhett abruptly stands, throwing his cloth napkin on the table.

"Help me," I mouth to Finley.

"I'll go fix us some more drinks," she excuses herself.

Our meal comes, but Rhett doesn't come back to the table. Finley finally returns, with no sign of him with her. She nonchalantly lifts both of her shoulders.

The judge methodically converses with Luther, acting as if he's truly interested in him when I know he's digging for more information.

"Did you sign up for the dance competition?" James has been quiet, listening to conversations.

"We did," Luther chimes in, wrapping his arm around my shoulder.

"How about you?" she asks Finley.

"I signed up with Rhett." She cuts her gaze at me and then back to James.

"You are going to be my dance partner tonight." The judge taps James on the shoulder.

"I'd rather not," she grumbles.

"Please," he says, and she caves.

"Fine."

The MC comes back on and announces the rules and the voting that will be done by the guests. They can mix and match partners at any time. "The first dance will be the cha-cha. Find your partner and meet on the dance floor."

"I don't know that dance," Luther stammers.

"It's alright. Audrey can dance it well enough for the two of you."

Scanning the room, I see Finley walk over to Rhett, who has his back pressed against the wall with his arms folded over his chest, take his hand, and drag him onto the dance floor. I'm honestly surprised he didn't leave.

The music comes on, and I don't know which

move Luther thought was dancing, but he's horrible at it. His body is stiff like a robot. "Loosen up your arms."

His first step comes crashing on my toes, and I wince. "Sorry," he says.

"I'll lead, you follow." He's not good at that, either.

The dance judges walk around tapping people out according to what the guests collectively vote on. An elaborate voting system was downloaded onto their phones when they purchased their tickets for the gala. It works like it does on television, instantaneously.

I'm shocked that Luther isn't tapped out in the first dance. He's wringing wet with sweat and panting.

"The next dance will be the foxtrot," the MC announces when the music stops.

As the music begins, Luther is tapped on the shoulder. "I was just getting the hang of it." He frowns.

By no means does he have any dancing skills.

"You've been matched with number twelve," the man tells me.

I look for the numbers pinned to us when we

signed up. My heart stops when I see the number on Rhett's tux.

He rocks his head from side to side as if he's struggling to contain his frustration. His jaw is clenched when he reaches me, extending his hands. The air around him is charged with heat and anger. I mirror his movements, and we synchronize seamlessly to the dance.

"I can explain if you'll just give me a chance."

"You lied to me." The force of his moves has me lightheaded. Either that, or it's the close proximity of his body to mine.

"I knew you were my father's friend, and you wouldn't have even given me the time of day if you knew I was his daughter."

"You're right. I wouldn't have." He spins me around, and I land firmly on his chest.

His response pisses me off. "So, what? Now you think I'm too young for you?"

"I never said that," he growls.

"I hid the truth because I was drawn to you."

"It doesn't matter. He warned me away from his daughters before his invite to the gala. He's protective of you."

"Do you do everything you're told or just when it applies to me?"

"You're the one that lied. Not me! You have the guts to be mad at me when you're the one on a date!" He spats the last word.

"It's business, nothing more."

"You planting a kiss on his cheek didn't look like business to me."

"I did it to piss you off. Why didn't you just leave?"

"Because as much as I hate it, I'm drawn to you too." The music stops, and the crowd erupts in cheers.

"The winner of tonight's contest goes to Audrey Steel and Rhett Fox. You two sure know how to tear up a dance floor." The MC waves a trophy in the air.

"I'm out of here!" Rhett storms off.

"Wow. There was pure heat coming off the two of you," James says.

"Did I miss something," the judge's brows draw together, making a V shape between his eyes.

"This is all your fault." I gnash my teeth. "You and your stupid rules to live by. I can't take it anymore." I push past him and grab my shawl.

"Where are you going?" Luther snags my arm.

"I'm sorry. I'm not feeling well. I'll send you the information, and we can discuss it in further detail after you've made a decision."

"I can drive you home."

"Thanks, but no. I just want to take something for my headache and lay down."

"I'll call you tomorrow and check on you."

"Please stay and enjoy the rest of your evening."

I rush outside into the pouring rain, kicking off my heels.

"I'll get your vehicle, Ms. Steel," the valet attendant says.

"No need, just give me the keys and tell me where it's parked." I hold out my hand palm up.

"The storm has blown in, and it's raining really hard. You should stay under the awning."

"I don't have time to argue with you. Just give me the keys."

Chapter 14
♥ RHETT

"HOW COULD I have been so damn foolish with my heart?" The glass of bourbon breaks and drips down the wall when I throw it in one full swing.

I rip out of my wet tux jacket and toss it on the ground. Kicking out of my shoes and socks, I drink directly from the bottle, pressing it painfully hard to my lips. I walk over to the leather couch that was delivered two days ago and stare down at it. "I have to get rid of you."

"Rhett, it's Audrey. Please let me in." She pounds on the door.

"Go away!"

She knocks louder. "I'm not going anywhere until we talk."

"I have nothing to say to you!"

When I saw her standing there in that dark green dress tonight, I wanted to haul her into my arms and make love to her. She's twisted my guts apart. I'm angry at myself for still wanting her so badly.

"If you don't let me in, so help me I'm going to kick down your door."

I can't squelch the clawing need for her despite who she is.

"You have to the count of three."

Her determination strips away my defenses.

"One! Please don't make me injure my foot."

I drag myself to my feet.

"Two!"

Inhaling sharply, I grab the doorknob and yank it open just as she says, "three." She's drenched with her hair falling down on her shoulders and rain-drops staining the silky material of her dress. Her nipples are embedded into the material, and my dick combats with my boxers.

She blinks the rain from her long lashes. "I'm so sorry." Her bottom lip quivers.

"You lied to me."

"Yes." She swallows.

"I don't trust you."

"I wouldn't either," she sobs.

I run my hand through my hair and clasp my hands behind my neck. "You were truthful about one thing."

"What was that?"

"You told me the first day I met you, you'd break my heart." I drop my hands to my side and turn my back to her, leaving the door wide open.

I lean on the counter with my fingers stretched wide, and I hear the click of the door closing. "And you said you'd never break mine."

"I guess that makes me the liar then."

Her footsteps bring her around the counter to look me in the eye. "It doesn't have to be this way."

"Yes, it does. I'm no good for you or anyone else."

"I don't agree."

"You don't have to. It's just the way it is."

She cautiously moves to where I'm standing, turning off her ringing phone and tossing it on the floor. "What happened to you?"

"It's not important."

"It is to me." Her hand shakes when she reaches to touch my face.

"You're soaking wet. You need to get out of those clothes."

"So are you," she whispers.

"I have a long shirt you can slip into and a pair of sweatpants." I stomp to my bedroom and snatch open drawers, finding what I'm after. "You can use

173

my bathroom and change into these." I toss the clothes to her.

When she closes the door, I slip out of my wet slacks, change into a pair of lounge pants, and make my way to the couch, waiting for her.

She comes out in a shirt that's four sizes too big, and it falls around her knees. I notice she didn't put on the sweatpants. She inhales when she sits on the couch, drawing her knees under her chin and tugging the shirt down. "You don't have on a shirt... or shoes," she adds.

"And you don't have on underwear, so I'd say we were even."

"Fair enough." She bites her bottom lip. "Why do you choose to be alone?"

"Because of the things I've done." I exhale.

"We've all done things we're not proud of."

"It's unforgivable." I let my head fall to the back of the couch.

"Tell me," she says quietly, touching my hand.

I bend forward with my elbows on my knees and my fingers to my chin, rocking back and forth. "My platoon got sent into a village in Afghanistan to take out a terrorist who had killed several soldiers, and women and children in his town."

"Sounds like a bad guy."

"He was. I was assigned to be the one to take him out. My men guarded me so I could get close to his house. He started firing on us. I got close enough to look in a window bearing no glass, and I could see his three teenage boys and his wife inside. I yelled for him to get them out of the house. A few minutes later, they came out the front door with their hands in the air, and he remained inside. As soon as they cleared the house, he started firing again. I couldn't get a good aim on him, so I yanked a grenade from my belt and pulled the pen. When I tossed it inside, I saw the boys sneak in the back door. There was nothing I could do to stop the explosion. I blew up three innocent boys." I've never been able to say the words out loud without tears running down my cheeks. This time is no different.

"It wasn't your fault," she says with a tear-filled voice.

"I've been told that a million times by my therapist, and yet, I've never believed it. It was my job to see to it that it was him and him alone."

"That's why you coach the boys."

"It's my way of making up for what I've done, as if coaching a hockey team will bring them back." I hang my head.

She crawls off the couch and maneuvers her

frame between my legs. "You are the best person I know. How could you possibly think you wouldn't be good enough for someone to love you?"

"It's been so long since I've felt anything but emptiness and remorse inside my chest."

"Let me love you, even if it's only for one night."

I can concede the war with her or lose the battle. I choose the latter. My mouth crashes against hers, mauling her lips, and my body comes alive. I want her so badly it hurts. I burrow one hand through the back of her damp hair, and the other wraps firmly around her waist, hauling her into my lap. She opens her mouth to me as hungry as I am, sweeping her tongue inside and exploring every line of my mouth. A moan slips from my throat, and I tug at her hair, drawing her closer. She's intoxicating like I knew she would be. I suck her tongue, and she presses her hard nipples to my bare chest.

Heat courses through my veins, and I change the tempo from warm to spiraling hot. I gnaw on her bottom lip while my hands find their way underneath her shirt. Her hands latch onto either side of my face, and she kisses me senseless, making me forget my own name. In this moment, she belongs to me and I to her. She flipped a switch in me that had been long forgotten. My body tingles with desire. I kick the coffee table out of the way and take her to the floor, laying her beneath me. She whimpers and lets her head fall to the floor, rolling it to the side, giving me full-on access to the skin beneath her ear. Her nails dig into my flesh with a feeling of rough desperation. I rain long, open-mouth kisses and love bites down her collarbone while pushing her shirt above her breasts. They are perfect, just like I knew they would be.

I support my weight on my left hand and brace her leg around me with another, earning another sweet groan from her lips.

She reaches down, dragging her shirt over her head. "I'm so glad I ditched the panties tonight." Her face is flushed.

My rough, calloused hand squeezes her thigh.

"Harder," she groans.

I apply enough pressure that it will leave a mark, but she knew that when she demanded I be firmer.

She fumbles with the string on my pants, and when she finally unties it, she shoves the material over my hips, down my ass, and pushes the rest of it off with her feet.

Taking her mouth again, we find a sweet, torturous rhythm that has her arching into me. I release her mouth and travel south, stroking the inside of her thigh with my thumb. Her chest rises and falls faster with each stroke. Rising to my knees to admire her, I lick my suddenly dry lips, and without her even touching me, I could come just looking at her.

"What?" she rasps.

"You are so damn beautiful."

"Shut up. I have better things you can do with that sexy mouth of yours." She guides my hand between her legs, touching her folds. It unleashes my primal instincts. I graze my teeth to her clit, and she hisses.

"Rhett," she pleads, pushing her hips upward.

"I'll take care of you. I promise." I slowly work my tongue inside her, sliding in and out. I add my thumb to the mix and stroke her, pressing deeper into her. She gushes with warmth in my mouth and I can taste her tension building. Stilling my thumb for a moment until she's relaxed, I sweep circles with it, caressing the parts of her that fill her with need. I reach up, cupping her breasts, and tweak her hardened nipples between my fingers, increasing her pleasure.

She arches her back and cries out. A powerful wave rolls over her body as she finds her release. When she gathers the strength to open her half-hooded eyes, all I see is love buried deep within them.

"I could watch you do that all day." I lower my head between her legs until she screams my name.

"Rhett!" Her fingers tangle in my wet hair.

When her body stops trembling, I climb up her body and kiss her, letting her taste herself on my tongue. Her hands run down my back and then sweep around my hips, taking my erection in her hand and firmly gripping it. I hiss air between my teeth, savoring her hands around my length.

"Audrey," I simply speak her name. I close my eyes, and she strokes me up and down, up and down. "That feels so damn good."

I let her continue for a moment before I pull her hand away. "Please tell me you're on the pill. I want to be skin-to-skin with you."

She smiles and nods.

"Thank god." My mouth waters as I run my hands over her perfect body. I slip my fingers between her legs again. "I love how wet you are for me." I curl my fingers, finding the spot that drives her crazy, and she rides my hand. I crash my mouth to hers and tug at her bottom lip and slowly sink my cock inside her, inch by glorious inch. Her hips start rocking, and I press my forehead to hers. I let out a moan when I'm fully seated inside her warmth, piercing my soul. I shift my hips slightly and begin thrusting in a deep rhythm, moving like we were made for one another. She wraps her long legs around my ass, pushing me deeper. We are both covered in sweat, with our hearts beating as one. I don't deviate from my brutal pace, taking me higher and higher with each thrust. My muscles tense, striving for an inevitable release. I slide my thumb between us, stroking her clit. I come apart the same time she does when my orgasm washes over me, rolling down my spine, drawing up my balls, and coursing through my cock.

Chapter 15
♥AUDREY

IN THE DIM light of the morning, he lies sleeping with small puffs of air blowing from his sweet lips. My hand shakes with the turmoil of emotions I'm feeling for him as I touch the soft whiskers on his chin.

"I'm going to love the hell out of you." My words are so soft they can only be heard and felt by my heart. "I only want to take your pain away, not add to it. You are so precious, and you deserve to be loved and forgiven, even if you don't believe it. You've got your demons, and I have mine. The inner workings of my life are in shambles, and I'm not sure how to love someone. You see, I've never been in love until I nearly kicked your door down last night. When you stormed out of the gala, I knew I had to go after you. My heart wouldn't allow for anything else. I want to tell you everything, but like you, I know deep inside of me you'll hate me for it. So, until the day comes that I don't have any other choice but to tell the truth, I'll live in my lies and protect you from them like the lioness I was trained to be. Your story was tragic and unbearable to you, and I'll do anything to ease the pain you've held for so long. My burden is unending by the choices I've made." *Do I regret them?* That's a deeper discussion, one that battles within me. "Though I appear normal on the outside, my life is anything but. I'm the true dichotomy of, 'appearances can be deceiving.'"

I curl my hand to hold my locket and feel the steady, slow gallop. "I love him, Momma. I'll keep him safe if it's the last thing I do in my life."

His eyes flutter open and immediately soak me in. He grips my hips, pulling me onto his hard body. I move my lips over his, savoring the texture and taste because I don't know if it will ever happen again. He inhales, parting his mouth, and I take full advantage, intensifying our kiss. He releases his firm grip on my hips, fisting his needy hands in my hair. I whimper, and the heat between us becomes explosive. I lift my ass and stroke him a few times, then, inch by inch, lower myself down on him. He lifts his head and sucks my nipple between his teeth. My breathing is sporadic, with my heart thundering.

My nipple is raw with need when he releases it. "Don't think so much. Just enjoy being in my arms."

Did he hear me talking? Does it matter in this moment?

"We'll sort out everything later."

"Rhett." I speak his name as if he owns me, and I'm ready to worship him.

He rolls us over, pinning me against the bed. I love the pull of his fingers in my hair, driving me crazy in the best way possible. He thrusts, and I start to shake. He covers my cries with his mouth, still rocking his hips into me, giving me no pause to escape my impending orgasm.

I cry his name again. "Rhett!"

"You're so beautiful," he utters against my swollen lips. When my legs finally relax, easing the muscles in my thighs, he raises slightly, cementing me with his milk chocolate eyes. "I mean it. You are gorgeous inside and out."

He wouldn't be saying those words if he truly knew, but the intimacy I feel from him has me believing him, if only for a moment in time. I pull his head to mine. "You talk too much."

He draws out every stroke until we come together. Our bodies arch together as if they were meant to be in rhythm...an alliance built on this day. He collapses on top of me and then rolls over.

"Damn."

I simply hold his hand and smile. This is what true happiness must feel like.

"Eventually, you and I are going to have to have a conversation."

And there it goes. A fleeting moment of blissfulness gone. "I know, but I like what we've been doing the last several hours a whole lot better." I keep my gaze fixated on the ceiling fan spinning round and round.

He rolls to his side, keeping our hands twined. "Your father is Judge Steel."

My head falls to the side, and I cut a narrow look at him. "You're telling me something I already know."

"He's going to have my balls for falling for his youngest daughter."

Tugging my hand free of his, I lean on my elbows and scooch until my spine is pressed against the headboard. "It's far worse than you can imagine. The judge doesn't let any man near his daughters."

"That's why three gorgeous, smart, well-educated women are still single." He sighs and joins me at the headboard.

"Are you crushing on my sisters?" I tease to lighten the mood.

"You were my second choice." He grins, and I hit him with the pillow.

"You're bad," I say, laughing, then squealing when he tickles me.

"I want to spend the day with you." He hushes my squealing noises with a kiss.

I lift my head, putting the pillow behind my head with my elbow sticking out. "It is Sunday. What did you have in mind?"

"Besides the obvious." He presses his hard cock into my hip. "What do you say we go to the beach?"

"I love that idea, but the only thing I have to wear is my soaking wet long dress from last night. I'll have to run home."

"I don't like that idea. You may not show up. I'll go with you."

"That's a hell no. The judge doesn't like anyone visiting our house, and if you showed up with me, this thing between us would be over." I wave my finger around.

"We'll stop and buy you clothes on the way."

"Again, all I have is your T-shirt to wear."

"Slip on a pair of my shorts."

"They'd fall off. But for you, I'll go in the T-shirt."

His chocolate eyes grow wide. "You don't have any underwear on."

"It won't be the first or the last time I've been pantyless."

"Stop, you're making me harder."

I toss the sheet back and climb out of bed. "Do you mind if I use your shower?" My bare ass sways from side to side as I walk into his bathroom, not waiting for an answer.

"Like hell you're showering alone." His bare feet slap the wood floor.

I'm deliciously sore from the shower. Rhett likes it rough. I didn't know I was so limber. Shimming into his oversized shirt, I peer over my shoulder and into a mirror to see the handprint he left on my ass.

He watches me and grins. "I like your butt cheek pink."

"Yeah, well next time, it will be my hand finding your fine ass."

"I like that you're thinking there will be a next time. You know I hear real well even when I'm half asleep."

"You heard me." I breathe out, and my head falls between my shoulders.

"I especially liked the part where you said you were going to love the hell out of me. The thing I find torturous is that you can't be truthful with me." He sits on the edge of the bed, leaning on his knees, and folds his hands together, peering at the floor.

"I'm sorry. I wish like hell that I could."

"I don't like it one bit, but I'm willing to accept it for now, as long as you're honest about how you feel about me."

I get down on the floor in front of him and tug at his chin. "I promise you with all my heart and on my mother's locket that you'll know how I ache for you." I wrap his hand around the locket.

"Let's go live in a bubble on the beach today. Tomorrow will come soon enough, and I have a feeling a lot of things are going to change." He presses his forehead to mine.

Arm in arm, we walk out together, and I get a few harsh stares when I walk into the beach store barefoot and dressed only in a long T-shirt. Rhett immediately finds the bathing suit rack and holds up a suit he likes.

"Every man on the beach would have a hard-on

with you walking around in this one." He laughs and tucks it in between two suits.

I sassily march over and take it out. "Then that's the one I want. Just think how lucky of a man they'll believe you to be." I sling my hair over my shoulder and slide the curtain open to the dressing room.

As I slip on the skimpy gold, shimmery bottoms, I see Rhett's feet, and then his hands grip the bar the curtain rests on. "You are going to be the death of me, aren't you? I've survived snipers' targets, grenades, land mines, and full-on enemy attacks. But you..." He doesn't finish his sentence, and I hold my breath, knowing he's right. His feet disappear, and I hear him walking away.

Tying the string around my neck, I adjust my breasts underneath the gold sequins and snatch my shirt, running out to find him. He's standing in the front window, staring out.

"Rhett," I say his name cautiously.

When he turns to the sound of his name, I swear there are tears in his eyes. He brushes them off. "I knew I was right about that suit." Chocolate eyes sweep the length of my body.

"I'm going to go pay for it." I hike a thumb over my shoulder.

I toss my charge card on the counter and tear off the tag hanging from a string.

"I guess you don't need a bag." The young girl behind the counter smirks.

Rhett takes my hand, and we walk the white sandy trail down to the beach. "Are you okay?" I shade my eyes to look up at him.

"You take my breath away."

"Was that the end of your sentence earlier?"

He nods. "I'll race you to the water." He jogs off before the word water leaves his mouth.

I laugh, feeling like the young girl I was never allowed to be, chasing after him. I leap and end up on his strong back. His biceps flex, holding on to my legs. "You cheated." I bite the rim of his ear.

He flips me over his shoulder, and I submerge myself in the warm, salty water, and a wave pulls me under. I come up beaming, loving how I feel with him.

"You might want to cover your left breast." His grin is wide and has to be hurting his face.

I look down, and sure enough, my girl escaped the flimsy material.

"Not that I mind. I prefer you topless."

"Coach Rhett!" I hear in the distance.

He splashes in the water, turning to the voice.

"It's Nelly and Filapose," he says.

They're breathing hard when they stop at the water's edge. "We need two more players." Nelly points to a volleyball net.

"So much for our day alone at the beach," he mutters.

"Hey, it's okay. As long as we're together, that's all that matters."

Rhett holds out his hand, and we follow behind them. They whisper and grin between them.

"They are talking about how hot you look in that bathing suit."

For the first time in my life, I want to cover up. "They're teenage boys," I say quietly. "I should have bought a cover-up.

He laughs. "I'll grab my T-shirt."

He tosses it to me, and I pull it over my head, then point to a bench nestled among the palm trees. "See that spot over there?"

He shields his eyes from the brightness of the sun. "Yes."

"That's my favorite place. I love watching the tide roll in and the sunset light up the sky."

"It sounds like a place of peace for you." He tugs my hand, and we walk in the white sands of the ocean.

I meet the rest of the players. They're sweet kids but a little mouthy with each other. Growing up with sisters is a lot different than hanging out with these boys. One of them swears, and Rhett handles it just by giving the kid a sideways stare.

"Sorry, Coach and Ms. Coach."

I can't help but smile. "It's Ms. Coach's turn to play." I hold my hands out, palms toward the sky and wiggle my fingers for him to give me the volleyball. "I might not know how to shoot a puck, but I can sure handle a volleyball."

We play for hours until my face and arms are sunburnt. Rhett and I kicked their butts, and I have to admit, it was a lot of fun. The afternoon storm clouds start to roll over the water, so we pack things up.

"It was a good day." I curl into Rhett's side.

"One of the best." He smacks a kiss on my salty scalp.

"What I'd give for every day to be like this. No worries in sight. A hot man in my bed and a day on the beach."

"I liked having you in my bed." His voice is gravelly and low, so the boys don't hear him. "They liked you," he adds, louder.

"They worship you, and for good reason. You

give them someone to look up to that has integrity and compassion. That's rare in my book."

"What do you say to me cooking you dinner?"

"I'd love to say yes, but I really need to get home. I've got some things I need to work out for tomorrow."

His feet dig solidly into the stand, stopping. "You aren't going to see Luther again, are you?"

"I told you, he's business. Nothing more."

"I don't like the way he kept eyeballing you."

"And how was that?"

"Like a hungry man, and I'm an expert on that look." He wraps his arms low around my waist with his hands landing on my ass.

"Your words match the look in your eyes." I stand on my tiptoes, softly kissing his lips.

"Then stay the night with me again."

I draw the corner of my bottom lip between my teeth. "I'll come over later. That way, I can grab a change of clothes."

"I kinda liked you running around in my T-shirt. The no underwear part came in handy." He waggles his eyebrows.

"I'll keep that in mind."

"Good girl." He smacks me on the ass. "Go home, do what you need to do, and I'll be waiting for you."

"You're incentivizing me." I'm enjoying our playfulness. It's something I've never had with a man.

Reluctantly, I drive home, but my smile is plastered on my face so hard it hurts...until I see my sisters pacing the living room floor.

"Where have you been? I've been trying to call you all day," Finley snaps.

"I turned my phone off. What happened?"

James grips me by the elbows. "Jack showed up at the house last night drunk, waving a gun around."

I gasp, covering my mouth. "No."

"There's surveillance footage from the outside cameras." Finley hits play on the remote that's transmitted to the large wall-mounted television screen.

I stand between them, watching. Jack is stumbling and slurring how much he loves me, and if he can't have me, nobody else will while waving a gun in the air. "Did you call the police?" I know the answer to my question. Police aren't allowed on Steel property.

In the video, I see the judge standing in the distance, smoking a cigar, watching it all play out while Finley deals with Jack, convincing him to leave.

"I drove him home." Finley hits pause.

"I'll go talk to him."

"You can't," James says sharply, then diverts her gaze to the ground.

"Why not?" Fear envelops my stomach, sending a shiver down the length of my spine.

"He was found with a single gunshot wound to the head. The police report says it was self-inflicted." Good thing Finley has a hold of my arm because my knees give way, and she catches me.

"Jack wouldn't kill himself," I choke out with tears flooding my eyes.

The judge strolls into the room. "You never know what a lovesick man will do." His voice is deep and foreboding.

"You did this, didn't you!"

He lifts a shoulder. "He came onto my property wielding a gun, threatening my daughter, but that's not an admission by any means. Never forget a lion protects its cubs." His voice teeters on the brink of menacing.

I boldly storm to within a foot of him. "If I find out you killed him, I'll turn you in myself!"

He lets out a huff. "This is your fault. You led him around on a leash for years. How did you think he'd react when you finally cut ties with him?"

Guilt nearly crushes me, but anger is at the forefront of my emotions. "You son of a bitch!"

"Call me what you want. I protect this family. I want to know where the hell you slept last night."

My head spins. He can't find out about Rhett. "I was reining in our prey."

"You bolted on Luther at the gala." He cocks his head to the side.

"I met up with him later and made up for it. My head was killing me, and I needed some fresh air."

"Your charity brought in ten million dollars last night."

Tears shred my cheeks. "Jack is dead. I couldn't care less about the charity." I run to my bedroom, slamming the door and falling onto the mattress. Shambles jumps from the dresser next to me and cries. I tuck her into my side and sob on the spot between her ears.

"I didn't love him, but he didn't deserve to die," I cry against her soft fur. My father is right; this is my fault. Even if I had loved him, the judge would have seen to it that he wasn't part of this family.

"Rhett." I sniffle his name. "I'll ruin his life," I mutter, and crawl out of bed, slipping on a pair of shorts, a clean shirt, and flip-flops and carrying Shambles snuggly in my arms.

Chapter 16
♥ RHETT

"WHY ARE you not answering your phone?" I grit. I've texted her with no response and called her twice, only to get her voicemail. I repeatedly plod the length of my apartment, ripping my hand through my hair in frustration.

"I don't even know where the hell she lives." I find my phone and Google Judge Ben Steel's name. It doesn't list a home address. After hours of pacing, I settle on the couch. "She changed her mind. She said she'd break my heart." I close my eyes, recalling the words she spoke softly this morning when I was half asleep.

"I want to tell you everything, but like you, I know deep inside of me you'll hate me for it. So, until the day comes that I don't have any other choice but to tell the truth, I'll live in my lies and protect you from them like the lioness I was trained to be. Your story was tragic and unbearable

to you, and I'll do anything to ease the pain you've held for so long. My burden is unending by the choices I've made."

"What could be so horrible I'd hate her? And what lies? If she's the lioness, that would make Ben the lion head." I believed her when she said she'd be honest about her feelings for me. Her family is so tight-lipped. What do I really know about them? Ben never gives much away. Our conversations are kept to golf, cigars, coffee, the weather, and how proud he is of his daughters for having good careers, but nothing personal other than I know his wife died many years ago, and he has raised his daughters on his own.

"Though I appear normal on the outside, my life is anything but. I'm the true dichotomy of, 'appearances can be deceiving.'"

"What did she mean by that?" I rest my cell phone on my forehead. I see her heart. She showed more of herself today, watching her with the kids. Her smile was the biggest I'd ever seen. I felt her in my arms and how much she's capable of loving. "I have to find out what she's hiding. She knows my demons and accepted them. Whatever hers are, I'll do the same for her, but she has to be honest with me."

My phone pings.

I'm sorry. Last night and today was beautiful, and I'll never forget how it felt to be held in your arms and making love to you, but it's over. I promised I would love the hell out of you, and this is my way of doing so. We can't be together. It will never work. My father won't allow it, and I know that sounds childish, but you don't really know him at all. Please don't call me again.

"She's afraid of her father." My gut churns as the realization hits me. "What kind of hold does he have on her life?" I rub my chin so hard it leaves it chaffed. "I need answers, and I'm not going to let this go." I stand. "This is my way of loving the hell out of you," I repeat her words. It's taken me years to find a woman I want in my life. I'm not letting her go without a fight.

I shower, trying to ease my tension, but it does no good. Toweling my body off, leaving my hair dripping wet, I throw on a pair of joggers and tennis shoes, running out the door, along the sidewalk, and crossing over a few blocks until I hit the beach. I don't break stride until I see her sitting on the bench under the palm trees, stopping in the thick sand when I'm a few feet from her, sucking air into my lungs. "I thought I'd find you here." I inhale deeply.

She doesn't look at me. "I sent you a text."

I wipe the sweat from my brow on my shoulder and sit, staring at her for a moment. The cat she's stroking vacates her arms and moves to my lap. "Who do we have here?" I take up petting her where Audrey left off.

"Shambles. Tiny traitor," she adds.

I chuckle. "Is her name a representation of what you think your life is?"

"It fits it rather well." A single tear streams from the corner of her eye, and she quickly swipes it away with her fingertips.

"Why are we over before we've even begun? And why are you afraid of your own father?"

"He's a lion among men. Being a daughter of Judge Steel comes with its own set of consequences."

"I'm not sure what that means. From the conversations I've had with your father, he adores you."

"You see what he wants you to see." She whips her head in my direction. "I've said too much."

Do I push her? "Tell me what happened."

She sucks in a shallow breath, almost as if her chest constricts, making it hard to breathe. "A friend of mine"—she swallows hard—"committed suicide."

I get the feeling she chose her words wisely. "I'm so sorry." I place my hand over hers that has a steel grip on her knee, and Shambles dips her head, rubbing it on her leg. "Is there anything I can do?"

She shakes her head and forms a flat line with her lips.

"It's hard to lose someone you care about, especially by suicide."

We sit in the quiet—other than hearing the wind weaving in and out of the palm trees.

"I know you're hurting, but what does the death of your friend have to do with us?" I ask gently.

She clears her throat. "He was someone I slept with for years."

Her confession stings. "Were you in love with him?"

"No," she responds quickly, brushing away another tear. "It was just sex for me."

I catch her drift. "But not for him."

She gets up abruptly, and Shambles jumps to the sand. "I can't do this," she says, her voice breaking at a high pitch.

"By this, you mean...love the hell out of me," I use her words.

"Believe it or not, this is me doing just that!" Swells of tears rain down her cheeks like a floodgate has been opened.

I get to my feet, easing my hands to her shoulders. "Please help me to understand why you're walking away from the best thing that's ever happened to me."

Her fingers tremble, touching my chin. "Who you think I really am on the inside is in a battle with what you see. You wouldn't understand."

"Try me." I'm on my emotional knees, pleading with her.

She stands on her tiptoes, branding me with a kiss. "Goodbye, Rhett," she says raspingly, with tears choking her.

Her whisper rips through me louder than the air sirens that sounded before a raid. "So you're just going to concede the battle," I say as she stoops over, picking up the cat.

"Think of me as nothing more than a green-eyed heathen that can't give her heart to anyone. We had a good time, nothing more."

Flashbacks of her in my arms assault my every emotion. "That's not true. The intensity between us last night was borderline frightening."

"A warrior chooses her battles, and that's what I'm doing."

"You're only at war with yourself...not me."

Her eyes rock back and forth with mine, and she clutches her necklace. "I wish with all my heart things could be different, that I really had a choice because I'd pick you a million times over."

"Then do it. Pick me, and I'll stand by your side no matter what."

"If that were only true." She exhales. "Regardless of what I want, there are other forces at play."

"Your father. I'll talk to him."

She shoves her hand in the middle of my chest. "No! You need to end your friendship with him. Please don't ask me why, just do it."

I take a step back, shoving my fists in my pockets. "If you think I'm the kind of man who doesn't know how to fight, you don't know me at all."

"You'll lose if you provoke him, and that's exactly what you'll do if you tell him how you feel about me."

"Then we'll keep us a close-guarded secret. Just please don't walk away." I see it in her eyes the moment she relents, and I fold her and her cat in my arms. "I love you even with all your secrets."

The cat tucks its head between our chins and purrs. "She likes you," Audrey sniffs.

"Smart cat." I chuckle to break the tension.

"You have to promise me to not mention my name around my father. I'd prefer you steer clear of him, but he might get suspicious if you do. He knows you left before me at the gala last night, and he wanted to know where I spent the night."

"What did you tell him?"

"Someone else's bed."

"I hate the sound of that."

"Me too. You're the only man I want holding me."

"I don't care about your past, but I won't be sharing you with anyone."

"You don't have to worry about that, no matter what you might hear."

"I want you in my bed."

"I can't. I have to go home." She slowly draws

herself out of my arms. "I have unfinished business to attend to. I'll call you when I can." I watch her take the dimly lit path to the parking lot.

"What the hell has Ben tied her into?" I don't know, but I'm going to find out.

I jog the distance back to my apartment and spend half the night researching Benjamin Steel. His record as a judge is impeccable. It's rare that a first-year attorney is offered a judgeship, but somehow, he accomplished it in record time, moving his family to Florida. I go back further, and there is very little information on him other than his wife died of cancer, and he was left to raise three young girls on his own. As far as the records go, he supported each one of them in their chosen careers. Finley is in the shadow of his footsteps. She was offered a judge position in the same court system, but she turned it down.

"Why would she keep the brakes on her career with her excellent reputation as an attorney?"

Researching the cases Ben has taken on, there's a vast majority of them having to do with financial corruption. Perhaps that's his forte. Finally giving in to fatigue, I close my laptop and climb into bed, texting Audrey before I turn off the light.

· · ·

I'm here for you when you want to talk. Sweet dreams.

Chapter 17
♥ AUDREY

TAKING OFF MY SHOES, the coolness of the marble floor hits the soles of my feet as I sneak into the house. As I make it to my bedroom door, I hear sobs coming from James's room. Shambles leisurely strolls to my bed and finds her spot on my pillow.

"Hey," I say softly, opening her bedroom door to see a light on in her bathroom. I tap lightly. "Are you okay?"

"Don't come in here." Her cry is desperate, leaving me no choice but to push my way inside.

"What's..." I gasp, not finishing my question when I see a pool of blood on her nightgown seeping into the floor around her. "Oh, my god." I rush to her side. "We need to get you to the hospital."

"It's too late. I've already lost the baby," she wails against my shoulder.

"I'm so sorry. Let me help you." Leaning over the garden-style tub, I turn on the hot water.

She gets to her feet with a blank look on her face.

She mechanically lifts her arms when I remove her gown, and I hold her hand as she steps into the bathtub. Her body trembles, watching through tear-drenched eyes the dark pink trail of blood streaming down the drain.

Reaching into a drawer, I take out a washcloth, dip it into the spray of the water coming out of the facet, and let the warmth drip down her spine. "You're going to be okay."

She wraps her arms around her knees that are drawn up to her chin, holding on tightly. "I wanted this baby so badly."

"I know you did."

"It's all my fault."

"No, it's not. Sometimes things just happen. You know this."

"It's my payback for the things I've done. What god would want me to be a mother?" Her cries grow louder.

"It doesn't work that way, sweetie. I crawl in the tub, fully clothed behind her, cradling her like a mother would.

"What's going on in here?" Finley peeks into the room and understands when she sees the floor.

"I lost the baby." James's shoulders shake.

Finley pulls out towels and mops up the floor

then sits on the edge of the tub. "I'm sorry you lost the baby." She lays her hand lovingly on James's head.

"She's shivering. We should get her dry."

"Should we take her to the hospital?"

"No," James snaps again. "I don't want our father to know anything, and I can take care of myself."

"Let's get her to bed," I say, standing, bringing James with me.

She stands stock-still as I dry the back of her, and Finley dries her front. Stripping out of my clothes, I wrap myself in a towel.

"I'll get her something to wear." Finley bolts out of the bathroom, and I walk James to her bed.

"Here." Finley tosses me a long T-shirt, and I dress James like a small child.

Finley pulls back the covers, and James gets in the middle, flopping to her side. I curl in behind her, and Finley goes to the other side, slipping beneath the sheets. The three of us hold each other, crying for the heartache James is going through.

I wish I knew what to say to her to ease her pain. She's held me many a night when I was a young girl crying for my mother. It's just one of many heart-breaking things we've gone through. She's strong, and she'll get through it, but I don't know if she'll ever be the same.

James finally cries herself to sleep, and we continue to lie next to her, giving her what comfort we can.

When dawn breaks through the blinds, I quietly slip out of bed so as not to wake her. Finley's spot has already been vacated. I'm greeted by Shambles outside her bedroom door, looking at me as if asking why the hell I wasn't in my own bed? I quickly dress once in my room, carrying Shambles with me.

"My sister needed me," I rasp as if she could understand me, then step over her to make my way to the kitchen, where I find Finley.

"Is she still sleeping?" she asks, pouring herself a cup of coffee.

"Yeah, I feel so bad for her."

"You feel bad for who?" The judge bounds in the kitchen, pulling on his suit jacket.

Finley and I share a look before she distracts him. "I heard you have a big day in court today."

"The end of a seven-day trial. I hope the jury finds the bastard guilty, or I'll have to overrule them."

"You're good at that," I say under my breath so he doesn't hear me.

209

"It will be a long day." Finley hands him his oversized coffee mug, but he pushes it away.

"I don't have time. I'll call Rhett to bring me several rounds."

My heart skips a beat at the mention of his name, wishing like hell they weren't friends.

He grabs his keys off the hook. "You, my youngest daughter, need to hurry up the process of bringing Luther to his knees, and I don't give a shit how you do it. Just get it done." The door slams shut behind him.

"He's in a mood," Finley gripes.

"When isn't he anymore? I swear the older he gets, the worse he is."

"I'm going to cancel my meetings today and stay home with James."

"Good. I'm glad because I can't. I want to get this Luther thing over with as much as he does."

"Do you have all your ducks in a row as far as the coin goes?"

"Yes, thanks to you. I'll have to find another way to break into his safe. I don't want James to deal with it."

"That's my job," her voice trails in the room, and we both twist around to look at her.

"I think your plate is full right now." Finley walks over to her, running her hand down her arm.

"I'll do it. It will keep my mind off of..." Her gaze falls to her stomach. "The baby I lost."

"We can handle it, so you can sit this one out," I reassure her.

"No. I need to do this and be done. I want to clean up my act, and then maybe I'll deserve a baby." I open my mouth to tell her differently, but her palm flies in the air. "I know what you're going to say, yet I've made up my mind about it. Please do me a favor and don't try to convince me otherwise." Her voice is raw and firm, along with her glare. It softens with her next words. "Thank you for taking care of me last night."

Finley and I wrap her in a hug. "It's what sisters do," Finley tells her.

"You'd do the same for either of us," I add, kissing her temple. "I'm sorry, I have to run. Luther will be in his office this morning, and I want to get this done."

The garage door opens smoothly when I press the button, backing out into the driveway. As I'm driving through town, I see Rhett on the sidewalk, striding to the coffee shop. It takes everything in me not to follow him inside. I want to believe with my whole heart that he'd stand behind me when he learns the truth. I'll wait and tell him when the situation with Luther is wrapped up so that I can tell him I'm walking away from our family business.

Turning into the parking garage, I find a spot on the second floor and take the elevator to Luther's office. His name is painted on the glass door. "This will be removed before too long," I say to myself and push through it to be greeted by his secretary.

"Do you have an appointment?" she asks, looking over her thick-rimmed red glasses.

"No, but if you'll tell him Audrey Steel is here, I'm sure he'll see me," I say with politeness yet with confidence.

She picks up her phone and buzzes him. "He said he'll be right out."

My heels click on the wood floor as I look around the office. He puts on a good show with the artwork displayed on his walls. A blatantly fake Picasso is perched above a faux leather couch. He thinks it makes him look successful. It says nothing but fraud to me.

"This is a surprise." Luther stands in a hallway.

"A good one, I hope." I smile and follow him into his office. "I told you I'd fill you in on a good investment, and now's the time to make your move." I slide the folder of information out of my bag and lay it on his desk.

He points to the chair for me to sit. "I take it your headache is better." He leans his hip against his desk and pushes a strand of hair behind my ear.

"Yes, thank you." I cringe on the inside and broaden my smile.

"Good, I'm glad to hear it." He hops up and moves around the desk, sitting to face me.

"I was hoping you'd let me make it up to you."

"And I will let you. What did you have in mind?" He smacks his lips.

"How about I bring dinner over to your house tonight, and I can plan on staying for breakfast."

"You sure do know how to persuade a guy." His gaze sickens me.

"The file has everything you need to decide if you want in on the coin or not."

He flips through the first couple of pages. "With your reputation, I don't think I need to dig any further. Sign me up."

I pick up the pen on his desk, handing it to him. "I'll need your signature on the last page along with the account number you'd like to move funds from to invest in the coin."

"No problem." He scratches his signature on the dotted line.

"Good. I'll have the account set up for you by the end of the day."

"I'll buy a bottle of champagne, and we can celebrate over dinner at my place tonight. I'll text you my address."

"I'll look forward to it," I muster in the sexiest voice that can possibly leave my lips under a full-on lie. I stand and pick up the folder, putting it back in my bag. "I'll see you this evening." I put an extra sway to my hips as I stroll out of his office and gasp in fresh air as soon as I leave the elevator. This part never seemed so hard when I was drugged out of my mind. Back in my car, I dig out the bottles from the bottom of my purse that I purchased from my dealer. "Just one wouldn't hurt." I have the cap open and a pill to my lips before I pause, thinking about James and her believing she doesn't deserve something good to happen to her because of her sins.

I hit the automatic button to roll down the window and spit the pill out. "We do deserve it. All of us." The engine roars to life with a single push of a button, and I peel out of the garage, leaving black skid marks in my wake.

Parking outside of the Bond & Bevel, I wait to get

a glimpse of Rhett coming from the direction of the courthouse. He smiles when he sees me sitting behind the wheel. Letting the window down on the passenger's side, he pokes his head inside with his arms propped on the door. "Hi. Do you want to join me for a coffee? It was a long night, and I need a pick me up."

His smile is infectious. "I could use a cup of joe."

He walks around, opening the door for me. I want to take his hand when he holds it out, but I think better of it. "Not in public," I say, unfolding my long legs from the seat.

He shoves his hands in his pockets, and we casually enter the coffee shop. "You look beautiful," he whispers next to my ear, then marches behind the counter to make our coffees personally.

"I'd love to see what other leather pieces you have," I say, not wanting to be obvious to everyone else that I want a moment alone with him.

"I'd love to show you, Ms. Steel." He hands me a cup and leads the way to his office. I reach behind me, close the door, and turn the lock. Rhett sets his coffee on his desk, and I toss mine in the trash, then lunge into his chest with my hands threading through his hair, crashing my mouth to his.

"A man could be upset that you threw away the

coffee he made you, but this more than makes up for it." His chuckle vibrates my lips as his hands pull my dress over my hips. "No panties again," he groans. He twirls me around and digs his fingers into my hips, setting me on the desk. With expertise, I unbutton his jeans and have his cock in my hands.

"I need you inside of me." Arching my back and spreading my legs, he swipes his fingers between my folds.

"You're wet," he moans a millisecond before he enters me in one hard thrust.

"Yes," I hiss, biting down on his collarbone.

He rocks his hips, and the feel of him deep inside me sends me spiraling into an instant orgasm.

"Damn it," he snarls, and his hips jerk. He holds me tight with his hands buried in my hair. "I'm sorry. I couldn't help myself."

"Don't be sorry. It's exactly how I wanted it to be."

Chapter 18
♥ RHETT

"YOU CAN STOP BY ANYTIME." I tuck my shirt into my jeans, zipping them.

She hops down, straightening her dress and then burying her face in my chest. "I won't be able to see you for a while. I'm going to be tied up with my job. There's an important investor I have to personally wine and dine. He's a bit needy."

"As long as his need doesn't include getting under your dress."

Her head pops up, and her stare bores into mine. "It doesn't. That's reserved only for you."

"Glad to hear it."

"I need you to trust me."

"You make it hard when you won't tell me the truth."

"I know, but it's for your own good, I swear."

"The boys have a big hockey tournament, not this Saturday but next. They've asked if I'd invite you."

I drape my arms over his shoulders. "What about you? Do you want me there?"

"Without question, and the last I checked, your father isn't into hockey."

"Did he say anything when you delivered coffee to him earlier?"

"I didn't see him. I left it with his secretary."

"Steer clear of him if you can. I can't stick around."

"I'd say I'd walk you out, but..."

"I'll call you," she says, waving on her way out the door.

"Perhaps I'm looking in the wrong place. Whatever is going on with the Steel family stems deeper than the surface." I sit behind my desk, open my laptop, and do a deep search into the family dynamics.

"Violet Steel." I read her name in an obituary. "I don't think he's told me his wife's name." There's a lawsuit related to her case. It says Benjamin Steel filed suit against the doctor and the hospital. The odd thing is it's dated five years after her death. "Why did he wait so long?" There's no outcome listed, yet the records show the hospital shut down not long after that. I Google the doctor's name, and he died the same year when his vehicle crashed into a tree on a dark road. "Hmm…" I find myself scratching my chin. "Whether he won the case or not, it seems in a roundabout way he got his revenge."

"Hey, boss man. Another order came in from the courthouse. They are wanting two boxes of coffee and some Danishes," the young barista hollers from the doorway.

"I'll take care of it." Shutting the laptop, I step behind the counter and fill to-go boxes with black coffee and a rectangular box with muffins and Danishes and dart out the door.

Security buzzes me in without question, and I head straight to the conference room, knowing that when boxes are ordered, it's where they want them delivered.

"Is that blueberry muffins I smell?" Ben laughs, walking into the conference room.

"Special delivery."

"I'm starving." He cracks his neck, stretching it from side to side. "It's going to be a hell of a day."

"These will have to hold you over until you get home. I'm sure your daughters will have dinner for you." I normally wouldn't mention his daughter's, but I want to figure him out.

"I don't know. Something's going on with the

three of them. Finley's pissy, James is quiet, and Audie…" he pauses with a chuckle. "That one has a date."

My stomach rolls. "Isn't she the one that's in finance?"

"Yes, and she's damn good at it too. She knows how to handle men."

Handle. Is she handling me?

"I don't expect she'll be home until morning. By the way, where did you disappear to the other night? You left in the middle of the gala."

"My tux was uncomfortable. I'm not used to dress-up affairs."

"I'd love to have a job that I didn't have to wear a damn tie." He tugs at the one around his neck.

"Do you ever think of having a different career?"

"Other than the attire, this one suits me fine. My wife is the one that encouraged me to become a lawyer. She saw something in me I didn't see in myself. Too bad she isn't around to see the man I've become." The wrinkles around his eyes deepen with sadness.

"I'm sure she'd be proud of all of you."

An odd look flashes on his face, and he purses his lips. "No doubt." He slaps me on the back. "I've got to get back into the courtroom. Thanks for the coffee and muffins."

"Anytime." His wife was his driving force. He must have derailed when he lost her, left alone to raise three girls. I'm more concerned at the moment that Audrey isn't expected home until the morning. "You're making it none too easy to trust you."

I find my way out and back to the coffee shop, spending the rest of my day ordering supplies and greeting customers just to try to keep myself from thinking about what Audrey is up to.

Chapter 19
♥ AUDREY

I LET myself into Jack's apartment with the key he gave me the first day he moved into this place. It smells of him. I almost call his name, forgetting that he's gone. Meandering through to his bedroom, I stop when I see one of my blouses on his unmade bed.

How many times did I show up here in the middle of the night high to use him? I sit on the edge of his bed. "I wish I was capable of loving you, Jack. You were always there for me when I called you, even when I was mean to you.

"I don't believe for one minute you took your own life." This has my father's name written all over it, just like the mysterious death of the doctor who failed to treat my mother. It wasn't enough that he'd already taken all his money. He wanted him dead. "The judge was never going to let you into our lives, and when you showed up threatening my life, he decided to end yours, and for that, I'm so so sorry. He was the reason I kept you at arms bay." I sigh.

"That's not completely true. I wasn't in love with you, and I know you never believed me even though I told you repeatedly, but you didn't deserve to die."

I sit in the stillness of his apartment for hours, regretting so many things in my life. I don't want Rhett to be one of those things. The possibility of a life with him warms my insides. He was right when he stated the intensity between us was almost frightening. I feel so alive when I'm with him, and the rest of the world doesn't matter. Neither do my crimes.

"One last time. One job to finish, and we'll all be free to live our own lives on our terms."

Losing all track of time, I jump to my feet when I realize I have only an hour to get to Luther's house with food in hand. As I drive, I order Thai food at a place not far from his house. Following the GPS, I arrive at a gated community. Checking the text he sent me, it gives an access code which I forward to James.

His residence is a modest two-story house on a corner lot surrounded by a six-foot white vinyl fence. Cameras are mounted on every corner. I make note of one by the front door and one on the side of the garage.

"What are you so worried about, Luther? You

live in a gated community." I tuck the bottle of pills in my purse, apply a layer of shiny pink lipstick, and head to his front door. Before I can knock, it swings open.

"I like a lady that's right on time." He smiles, kissing my cheek.

I hold out the brown paper bag. "I hope you like Thai food."

"It's one of my favorites." He opens the door wider and lets me inside, and I can feel his stare on my ass. Moving past him, there's an expensive chandelier lighting up the entryway and a real Picasso painting hanging on the wall.

"I see you're a man of exquisite taste."

"And you have an eye for art." He closes the door, and I feel the walls surrounding me.

I shake it off. "You have a lovely home." While his wife and children struggle to pay the rent. The Picasso will bring in enough money to more than meet their needs.

"I'm very proud of it. I have champagne on ice as promised." He holds out his hand in the direction he wants me to walk. He's a good con and a gambler. His house reeks of money.

"You can set the food on the counter. I'll pour the champagne.

When he has his back to me, I slip my hand inside my purse, unscrew the bottle, and take out four pills, gripping them in the palm of my hand.

He pops the cork, wearing a cheesy grin, and pours the bubbly into two tall glasses. Picking up one, he hands it to me. "Cheers." He taps the rim of my glass to his.

"Congratulations on your investment."

"I'll be expecting a big fat return." He sips his drink.

"Where might I find plates?"

"I'll get them." He turns to a cabinet behind him, and I plop the pills into his drink, swirling it around a few times, then top off both of our glasses.

"This is really good."

"It should be. It cost me over two hundred dollars." He smirks and straightens his spine, arrogance spewing around him.

"The insurance business has been good to you."

He walks around to me, tucking a piece of hair behind my ear. "It makes a modest living. The real money comes from investments and knowing how to work the system."

Like stealing from your clients. "Everyone cheats the system every now and then." I shrug a shoulder and twist away from him to fix our plates.

"I'm surprised a woman like you would understand." He chuckles.

I know more than you ever will in your pea-sized brain. "A woman like me?" I bat my eyes.

"Yeah." He picks up our plates, and I follow him into a formal dining room with a table that seats twelve. "You're sophisticated, intelligent, extremely beautiful, and a smart investor. There'd be no need for you to be morally gray." He pulls out the chair next to his on the end of the table.

I'm so far beyond morally gray. You'll find out tomorrow morning. "My father being a judge is a deterrent." I almost laugh at my own nonsense.

"I bet he'd be pretty scary and extremely hard on daughters."

"You have no idea." I sit, placing the napkin in my lap.

"Is he the reason you're not married?" He takes his seat and sips his champagne.

"Men find successful women intimidating...and there's my father."

"I find you fascinating." His cheesy grin is back. "I'd love to pick your brain on finances. I'm a bit of a gambler and damn good at it, so there's always excess cash for me to invest."

The bank account he shared with me to fund the

coin had over two million dollars in it. His safe must be bulging. I pick up my fork and take a bite of my shrimp Pad Thai. "I could be eager to take your money, but we've just initiated our first investment, and I like to prove myself before my clients go all in." *I'll have every dime of your money by this time tomorrow if not earlier.*

He taps his temple. "Smart woman. Gain their trust first. I operate my business the same way. Once my clients see what I can do for them, I can sell them a policy they don't really need, and I can manipulate the outcome."

Bastard freely admits it.

He stops with his fork midway to his mouth. "Perhaps I've said too much with your father being a judge."

Casually lifting my hand, I trace his knuckles with my finger. "Your secret is safe with me." I already know all your dirty secrets.

"Good, because I think you and I could have something really special." His eyes dilate, and it's everything I can do to not shove my fork up his nose.

"I think so too," I purr.

As we eat, the narcissistic asshole talks only about himself. He never mentions having children or an ex-wife. He goes on and on about the things he's done and how good he is at gambling.

"I think we should have another glass of champagne." He starts to stand, and I lay my hand on his shoulder. "Please, allow me."

"I love a woman that wants to wait on a man." His gaze skims my legs when I get up, and I purposely add more sway to my hips.

This is taking far too long. I snag a few more pills and watch them dissolve in the bubbles. Holding one between my fingers, I'm tempted to let it melt in my mouth. "No," I whisper harshly. "I don't want to do anything stupid."

I carry them back, and he's sitting sideways in his chair, tapping his thigh for me to sit.

Walking between his legs, I hand him his glass, then glide onto his lap, draping an arm over his shoulder and twisting the curls of his hair between my fingers, wanting to retch the entire time.

"Here's to a new partnership."

"I'll most certainly drink to that." He gulps his drink. "What do you say we take this party to my bedroom." His nose trails my jawline.

The drugs better work fast, or I'm going to vomit all over of him. "I'd like that." I stand. "Lead the way."

His smile is broad, twining his fingers with mine, leading me up the stairs by the Picasso I'm going to enjoy taking from him. When we make it to the top landing, he stumbles.

"I think the champagne is getting to me." He rightens his shoulders and spins me in his arms. "I perform better, drunk, if you know what I mean." He thrusts his hips to mine, and his erection is less than impressive. Leaning in to kiss me, I turn my head to the side and playfully drag him into his master bedroom. He sways and follows me.

Slowly, I unbutton my blouse, exposing my bright red lacy bra. Luther blinks a few times and licks his lips. "Stripping for me," he slurs.

"I thought you might like a woman who takes charge."

He waivers striding to me, and when I see his eyes close, I move out of the way, and he falls onto the bed.

"It's about time," I huff, buttoning my blouse.

Walking around to the far side of his king-size bed, I yank the covers down, climb in, and drag him into the middle of the bed. His shirt comes off easily, baring a patch of blond hair in the middle of his chest. He's firm but not muscular. Loosening his belt, I tug it through the loops, then work on removing his socks and shoes. Next, his pants. I've never been so reluctant to see what's beneath a man's pants. The zipper eases down, and I have to shift his body weight to remove the rest of his clothes.

"I guess your charm and money is what draws women to you because that thing couldn't please any woman." I toss the covers up to his waist.

"Now to get to work." Slipping out of my shoes, I jaunt the stairs to get my cell phone, dialing James's number. "Are you sure you want to do this?"

"Yes. I've been circling the neighborhood waiting for your call."

"He's out cold."

"I'll park down the street and be there in a minute."

"I'll text you when I've turned off the cameras."

"Okay." She disconnects.

I find his office on the first floor and the computer that operates his security for the house. Another skill the judge taught each of us is how to navigate around any security system. Putting it on a loop timer is the easiest thing to do, but I'm going to take his completely offline and cut the outside feed so he believes he was robbed; at least until I throw it all in his face. I love this part of the game when I make the bad guy cry.

Cutting the feed, I text James the all clear, and she shows up in the shadows wearing all black. She follows me inside the house. "You always look the part of the cat burglar totting two large duffle bags." I laugh quietly.

She smiles but it doesn't reach the corners of her eyes that are filled with sadness. "It's the perfect outfit to break into a safe." Her gaze sweeps the room. "He likes expensive things."

"That Picasso is going with us." I point.

"Finley will have a good buyer for it. Where's the safe?"

"Upstairs in his room where he's passed out cold." We pad up the steps to his room.

"He's never going to know what hit him." She smirks.

Opening his closet door, the safe sits against the far wall. James removes fine tools from her back pocket and gets to her knees, working on the lock while I explore his room. A massive oak dresser takes up one entire wall. Everything is meticulously in place in the drawers. The middle one has a velvety box with a glass lid displaying expensive watches.

"I'll take these," I say, lifting it out of the drawer.

A row of rings is shelved behind it. One diamond ring, I'm guessing to be five carats. "Who did you pilfer this from?" I hold it up, admiring it. "Probably one of your clients who died that you talked into leaving you their fortune."

"Got it," I hear James say, followed by a click of the lock.

"That didn't take you any time at all." I meander over to her, peering over her shoulder. "That's a lot of cash."

"Help me load it into the bags." She unzips one, and we start filling it with stacks of hundred-dollar bills.

"I think our friend Luther here has been doing way more than gambling. I found women's diamond rings in his dresser. He's been making friends with lonely old women who have no family."

"Getting them to leave him everything," she adds.

"That's my guess."

"I despise him more and more by the minute."

"At least you don't have to crawl in bed with him naked," I scoff. "You get off easy."

"I don't envy you, but this is the last time, right?" She tilts her head up to look me in the eyes.

"Yes. The Steel sisters are done, and we are all

going to go on and live happy lives. Fall in love, and you're going to have lots of babies." I run my hand over her hair.

She blinks a few times and purses her lips but doesn't say anything else until we've wiped him clean.

"Do you pack a gun?"

"Always."

"Be careful," she says before she walks out the door carrying both bags by the strap over her shoulders.

"I'll see you at the house in the morning." I settle on the couch, knowing Luther will be out for hours and watch old movies, wishing I was with Rhett rather than here.

Chapter 20
AUDREY

GLANCING at the oversized clock in Luther's living room, it's just shy of six in the morning. The drugs will be wearing off soon. Exhaling, I turn off the television, making sure to put the remote back where I found it. Like a sloth, I return to his bedroom. He's barely moved an inch, and there's drool leaking from the corner of his mouth.

I remove my clothes, leaving on my bra. He's the type of guy that would fumble with the clasps and work his hand beneath it. I lose the panties and tuck them under the pillow. A shiver runs down my spine, lying next to him, covering myself with the sheet, and placing my head on his shoulder.

Within minutes, he starts to stir. Moaning, he stretches and his hand falls to the middle of my back. "Good morning, beautiful." His voice is groggy.

"Good morning." I rub his stomach.

"Man, that must have been some night." He lifts

the sheets, exposing his lower body. "I don't even recall getting naked."

Rolling off of him, I climb out of the bed, slipping my panties back in place. "It was one wild ride." I grin over my shoulder.

"That champagne must have been exceedingly strong." He runs his hand down his face like he's trying to shake off his grogginess.

"It didn't help that we drank the entire bottle." I wiggle my ass as I get dressed.

He angles to his side and props up on his elbow. "Come back to bed."

"Sorry, I've got things to do." I purposely flip on the bathroom light to light up the room.

"Why is my closet door open?" He scowls, jumping out of bed, not bothering with his clothes.

"I don't know," I respond nonchalantly.

"What the fuck!" he yells, running into the closet. "All my money is gone!"

"What are you talking about?"

He frantically runs out of the closet and sees the dresser drawers askew. "I've been robbed!"

"That's not possible, we were sleeping right there." I point to the crumbled bed sheets.

He runs down the stairs, yelling about his cameras. I pad down behind him, and he's tapping furiously on the keyboard. "It's not working!" He bumps my shoulder, running past me and going outside. When he comes back in, he has frayed wires gripped in his hand.

"Whoever did this cut the feed!" he growls with his jaw tightly clenched. His gaze goes to the empty place on the wall where the Picasso hung. "My painting!" I swear, in his anger, he grew fangs.

"I'm calling the police. Where the hell is my phone?" His bare feet slap the floor as he barrels into the kitchen. He hits the buttons on his phone so hard he fumbles with it, dropping it on the floor. "Damn it!"

"Calm down."

"Calm down!" he repeats in a high pitch. "How the hell did we sleep through someone breaking into my house?" The phone is back in his fist.

"I wouldn't make that call if I were you." I tsk.

His gaze narrows on me. "Why not?"

"Because if you do, you'll be exposed for what you really are." I bat my eyes, drumming my nails on the counter, thoroughly enjoying this part of my job. "And besides, you don't want to be hauled out of your house by the cops completely naked." I curl my lip in disgust.

"You did this!" he seethes. "You set me up!'

I tap the end of my nose. "Bingo. You've been a very bad boy, Luther, and it's time you paid the price. You've robbed clients, not paying out policies. You've swindled little old ladies out of their life fortunes." I move closer to him and my purse, where my gun is tucked in a hidden pocket. "You've neglected to pay child support and left your ex-wife not only penniless but with a few broken bones."

"You bitch! You can't prove any of it!"

I snatch my gun from my purse, aiming it at his crotch. "That's where you're wrong. I can verify every word. Try fighting it, and I have a good attorney and a judge that will make sure nothing works out in your favor."

"I'll expose you," he grits.

"You'll do no such thing. In fact, this house will bring in a pretty penny. You can either give it to your wife, or you can sell it. That's the only choice you get to make in this situation."

"Why are you ruining me?" Defeat is laced in his tone.

"You bilked a grieving wife out of her husband's life insurance policy, falsifying the reason he died on the policy. Once you corrected it after the fact, you had the plan send the money directly to you, and she was none the wiser that you kept *her* money.

Don't try denying it. I'm good at what I do, and I have the proof locked away."

"I'll give her the money if that's what you want."

"What I want is for people like you to quit preying on the innocent and getting rich off of it. Better yet, the world would be better off with you ten feet under the ground."

"What are you? Some type of Robin Hood?" he barks.

"You say that like it's an insult. I'd be proud to use that title."

He takes a step toward me, and my finger lodges on the trigger. His hands fly out in front of him, and he falters back against the counter. "Don't," he stammers.

"Then I'd stay put if I were you."

"What's going to stop me from coming after you?"

"Well." I lift a single shoulder. "I can either pull this trigger now or later. If you come after me in any way or even mention my name, all the proof I have will be at my father's hands, and you'll spend the rest of your miserable life behind bars. And you being a pretty boy, I can guarantee you it won't be much fun. You'd be better off if he killed you."

"What else do you want from me?" His demeanor changes as his shoulders sag.

"That's more like it. You'll sign this house over to your wife and kids. You'll make restitution with the clients you've stolen from, and don't think there's not a list a mile long of your victims."

"How am I supposed to do that when you've taken all my money?" His eyes grow wide as saucers as realization smacks him across the face. "The coin. It wasn't real, was it?"

I shake my head. "How does it feel to be taken advantage of?"

"Like shit," he whines. "Please don't do this," he begs, pressing the palms of his hands together.

"As for your question, I don't care how you do it or if it takes the rest of your life, but you'll pay each of them back."

"I won't be able to afford to live."

"That's not my concern. What is, however, is that I will always know what you are up to. If you so much as think about stealing from anyone again, you'll find yourself in a teeny tiny cell with a room-mate that likes sandy blond men."

"This coming from a thief." He raises a brow. "What are you going to do with all my money?"

I keep my aim on him while tapping a finger to

my chin. "Back child support, generous charitable donations, paying back the people you stole from."

"Then why are you demanding I pay them?"

"Consider it the interest you owe them and then some."

I pick up my purse and back away. "Don't forget the promises I've made to you if you even think about mentioning me or my family to anyone."

"What's to keep me from leaving the country?"

"Money. You don't have any. If you happen to earn enough by gambling, then so be it. Leave the country. If I don't have to lay eyes on you again, the better off I'll be, and so will your boys you don't give a crap about, but they will be well taken care of without your presence in their lives."

"Why did you go to all the trouble to make it look like I was robbed?"

"Because the look on your face was priceless, but nothing compared to telling the truth." I slam the door behind me with great satisfaction and relief at the thought of this being my last time. A normal life is finally in my grasp.

The fatigue of being up all night finally sets in on the drive home. I want nothing more than a long, hot shower to wash the scent of Luther and to crawl into bed for the rest of the day. I know the judge will have other plans. He'll insist on a family meeting that might have even started already.

When I open the garage door, I see the Picasso painting leaning against the wall. Shutting it behind me, I get out and open the door leading to the kitchen, where, as I expected, the judge, Finley, and James are waiting for me.

"Great job." My father's large hand clasps my shoulder.

"He had over ten million dollars in cash in his safe," Finley says.

"Can we deal with the details later. I'm exhausted."

"You know that's not how this works," the judge huffs. "We go over everything in detail to make sure we didn't miss any steps to make sure Luther Craig is not a liability to any of us."

His tone grates on my nerves. "So, if he is, you can take care of him like you did Jack!" I snap.

"Watch your tone!" His brows form a V as he glares at me.

"None of it matters anymore," James steps in. "This is our last job."

"We quit." Finley anchors her hand on James's shoulder for support.

"Like hell you are." He chuckles.

We all three stand with our arms crossed, staring at him.

"Look, I know you're upset about Jack, and I went a little crazy when you told me you were pregnant."

"Was," James whispers.

He cocks his head to the side. "What?"

"I lost the baby." Her eyes fill with tears.

"I'm...I'm sorry." He looks sincere, with a crease deepening on his forehead.

She licks away the tears falling on her lips. "I don't want your pity. I want to be done with this mess and have a new life away from here...away from you."

"You don't mean that," he scowls.

"She does," I butt in, and so do I."

"I've given you girls everything."

Finley makes the first move toward him. "You have, and we appreciate everything you've done for us, but this is no longer our vendetta against the world. We all know how much our mother meant to you and that her death was devastating to all of us, but if she were still alive, can you honestly say she'd still love you for the man you've become or what you've turned us into?"

"She'd want us to be happy. Find men we could

fall in love with and have lots of children." I tuck my hand around James's waist.

"None of that matters because she isn't here!" His voice fills the room and then some.

"No, she's not, but she's alive in the three of us," James says louder this time. "I want her legacy to live on through our children, your grandchildren. Don't you want to see her beautiful features on a child's face?"

He falters with his back to the wall. "I miss her every damn day." He sucks in air, and just when I think he's caving, he stands tall, tilting his chin upward. "I will not give up my life's mission, and neither will any of you." He waves a finger between the three of us.

"What are you going to do if we refuse?" My gaze narrows hard on his.

James gasps. "You'd expose your daughters?"

"He's bluffing because he's tied to everything we've done," Finley snaps.

"I'll do whatever is necessary to keep the three of you in line." He raises a single brow.

"Unfreaking believable." My mouth gapes.

"He doesn't love us. We're nothing more than pawns in his game." James rasps like she's choking on her words.

"That's not true. I adore all of you, but this family sticks together. It's how each of you has been so successful."

"We've made our own wealth. None of the money we steal goes into our pockets," I argue.

"That's not true. Your collective educations were courtesy of the money we've stolen. This house, the cars you received as gifts growing up, even your status in this town was bought and paid for with vengeance money." He circles largely around the three of us. "Now, enough of this nonsense. I need details."

I take James's shaking hand in mine, and we leave him standing in the kitchen alone when Finley follows us out.

"Fine! Take a break. Get some sleep, and we'll discuss the details later!" he bellows.

"I'm late for work." James snatches the keys to her car.

"So am I." Finley follows suit, picking up her briefcase. "The plan hasn't changed because of his threats. We stick together." She hugs James.

They head out, and I want nothing more than to sleep for hours on end. I'm halfway up the stairs when my phone pings with a message from Rhett.

. . .

I need to see you NOW!

I'm utterly drained, down to my very core, but the idea of having him close, with his body pressed against mine, is far more enticing than the allure of sleep. After a quick shower and a change into a dress, I dash out the door, speeding into town and bounding up the stairs to his place with newfound energy.

I rap my knuckles on the door, and soon after, I hear the heavy thud of his footsteps. When he swings the door open, there's a palpable tension in his body that I can sense, although I can't quite pinpoint the exact emotion. It doesn't elicit warm and fuzzy feelings within me.

Chapter 21
♥ RHETT

"YOU SAID you needed to see me now." Audrey cautiously steps inside when I widen the opening.

I close the door behind her, remaining silent.

"What's wrong?" I flinch when she touches my arm. "Did something happen?" Fear rolls over her beautiful face.

I exhale loudly, shoving my hands in my pockets and stride past her, then turn around, glaring at her.

"Talk to me."

I swallow hard. "What were you doing last night?" I'm baiting her to see if she'll tell me the truth.

"I was working."

My laugh is more of a sneer. "Since when do you and James work together?"

Her eyes widen a smidge, and I'm betting the word shit is rolling around in her head.

"That bright yellow car of yours sticks out like a sore thumb. I was craving Thai food, and I took an Uber across town to one of my favorite restaurants."

She presses her lips together, not saying a word.

"I called your name, but you appeared to be so lost in thought you didn't answer me. I thought perhaps something was wrong."

"You followed me." All the air visibly leaves her lungs.

I nod, flattening my lips. "I had a conversation earlier in the day with your father, and he happened to mention you wouldn't be back until morning. When I saw you pull up to the gated community, jealousy hit me in the gut. I wanted to break down the barrier and chase after you. I tried to convince myself to leave, but I couldn't."

"It's not what you think."

"Just as I was about to have the Uber driver take me home, I saw James go through the gate. I followed in behind her and had the driver park a block down from her. She got out of her vehicle wearing all black, carrying two large duffel bags, and you opened the door for James." My jaw twitches as I step to within inches of her. "Here's the part where you decide our fate. Which will come out of your mouth? A truth or a lie?" My dark eyes rock back and forth with hers, willing her to be honest with me as anger bristles up my spine.

"I don't know if you can handle the truth." Her

words are soft.

"Try me." The muscles in my jaw flex.

"I want to tell you."

"I've told you my secrets."

"This is different. You won't understand." She moves around me and sits on the couch.

Instead of sitting next to her, I push the coffee table out of the way and drag the leather chair in front of her, sitting, leaning on my knees, folding my hands together. "Talk to me, Audrey," my tone dampens a tad.

"Remember the first day we met?"

"When you told me you'd break my heart." It's not a question.

"Yes." She pauses, licking her lips. "You asked me what I did for a living."

I cock my head to the side, trying to recall her words.

"I said I was a thief."

"You were kidding." I blink rapidly.

"I was telling you the truth."

"I don't understand." My brows furrow.

"You know my mother died of cancer when I was two. A cancer that could have been cured, but we were penniless. My father lost his job trying to take care of my mother. From what my sisters told me, he was so angry at the doctors because they wouldn't treat her, and he never got over it."

My heart softens, and I take her hand in mine.

"She was his lifeline. After she died, he went back to work and took classes at night, leaving my sisters the burden of raising me. He swore to my mother that he'd get us out of the trailer park and make a life for us. When he got the chance, he kept his word and moved us here."

"He's given his daughters a good life."

"The judge's anger evolved and grew talons, grooming us in his vendetta against all who are wronged. He made the doctor and the hospital pay for our mother's death."

"How does this play into what I witnessed last night?"

"The daughters of Judge Steel are thieves led by him. The seat he sits in allows him to find victims who've been wronged by someone, finding justice for them, and we help him."

I let go of her hand and lean back, running my hand over the scruff of my face. "You're a family of thieves."

She watches me as if trying to gauge my reaction to what she's disclosed.

My mouth twists, biting the inside corner of my

lip but saying nothing.

"It's the reason I never get close to anyone. You're the first person I've ever truly wanted." She raises her hand, cupping my cheek, and my eyes squeeze shut. "Last night was the last time. I'm walking away so I can have a life with you. That is if you still want me."

My eyes pop open. "Wanting you isn't the question. Every time I see you, I want to touch you. You make it hard for me to breathe when you're this close to me."

Her heated stare roams my body when I stand, moving to look out the window. I hear her get to her feet and feel her arms wrap around me, her front to my back. "You didn't throw me out."

I slowly twist in her arms, dropping my gaze to her mouth. I'm torn between adoration and my moral compass. "I don't know what to think or feel."

She lifts my hand to her heart. "Feel this. It's beating just for you." There's pure longing in her voice and eyes.

The things she's told me will ruin us, but right now, I don't care. I sweep her hair over her shoulder and rub my thumb over her bottom lip, wiping away her truth. I can feel her body heat up through the thin layer of her dress, making me hard.

"Say something," she rasps.

I open my mouth to speak, but my need for her is stronger than words. I spin her around, pressing her back to the window and jostling the panes. I capture her hands in one of mine at her lower back, holding her captive. She moans against my mouth, breaking any thoughts that this is a bad idea. Twining a single finger in the strap of her dress, I twist it down her arm and bite her sexy collarbone. The anger I was filled with only moments ago is replaced by lust for this woman.

She arches her back, pressing her peaked nipples against my chest. Every nerve ending in my body rages to life, and it feels like I'm on fire.

"I want you so badly," she hisses, breaching my last resolve.

Our mouths collide in a rush to devour one another, sweeping our tongues together hard and hot, losing control. My hand lets go of hers, grasping her ass and lifting her onto the windowsill. She puts the heel of her hands on the edge, giving her leverage, wrapping her legs around my waist, and locking her ankles. I frantically push her dress up to find her completely bare underneath. My mouth slides down her neck to her nipple, sensually assaulting it and making her moan. As one hand touches her clit, the other weaves through her hair to the nape of her neck, kissing her with the hunger I feel for only her. She reciprocates the need with a thrust of her hips, working my fingers inside of her.

"That feels so good," she purrs against my lips. Her hands are on my shoulders, my biceps, and then ripping my shirt off. She gasps sharply when my fingers toy with her most sensitive spot deep inside her, taking my time to draw out her pleasure. She nips at my ear, and my desperation for her climbs to new heights.

Dropping to my knees, I spread her legs and lick her entrance. Her fingernails dig into my shoulders, clawing at my skin.

"You taste wildly addictive." I suck and nip at her.

"Don't stop. I'll die if you do," she pants, pressing her hips upward to give me a better taste.

I capture her clit between my teeth and assault it with my tongue like a starving man while expertly using the friction of my thumb to apply pressure where my chin is rubbing her. She loses her leverage, and I ease her to the floor without stopping.

"You're so damn soft and wet," I murmur between laps of my tongue. I feel the sweet coil growing inside her. While keeping my mouth on her core, I insert my thumb, making tight circles on her already swollen clit.

"More!" she yells, shuddering.

"You're so hot." My voice sounds like it's been scratched.

She clamps her thighs tight around my head, and she mindlessly loses control, crying out my name. "Rhett!"

I lap up every drop of her before I move to get to my feet, removing my pants, then lying back down with my hips between her legs, framing my sweaty body over hers.

"I need you," she gasps, feeling the tip of my cock at her soaked entrance.

I'm nothing but ragged breath and full of hunger as she arches upward, and I push inside inch by inch.

"I need all of you," she rasps.

Shifting my hips, I give her what she wants, driving deep inside her, feeling a knot of pleasure building, tingling my spine, burning my veins.

I draw my head back, searching her eyes filled with want. A heartbeat later, she devastates me with a moan. My mouth clashes with hers, and I thrust my tongue with the same rhythm as my hips.

My chest rubs against her nipples, and she

hisses. "I need..."

"I know what you need." My teeth graze the sensitive skin of her neck as my hand trails between us, stroking her into another orgasm, and she comes apart. I hold tight, riding out the waves rolling through her, squeezing around my cock. Her thighs tremble as she comes down from her high, but hot and insistent need coils in my gut. The sensation of her fleeing orgasm has me shifting my hips, chasing after another one.

Our mouths meet for a quick taste of one another, and then I draw her knees upward, settling deep inside her. She moans. "That feels so good." Her skin is flushed, and her hair is damp as she locks her gaze on mine. I can't resist the spot under her ear, and she hisses when my teeth skim over it. The sound she makes and her panting pushes me into a hard, deep, unhurried rhythm that has her withering beneath me.

"Faster." She clutches my hips, digging her fingers into my skin.

My body follows her command willingly, and I thrust harder, barely holding on until a wickedly delicious grin tugs at her lips. My control snaps, and I roll my hips, spiraling, driving into her for my release, taking her with me.

Chapter 22
♥ AUDREY

THE FIRE inside my body is dampened when he presses his forehead to mine, keeping his weight on his arms framing my shoulders, and his chest rises and falls hard against me. My lips skim the plane of his jawline. "That was so powerful."

He lifts his head back enough to look at me. "Did I hurt you?"

"Quite the opposite." I playfully wiggle my hips. "I don't think I'll ever get enough of you." He rolls to his side, and I push him to his back, straddling him. Long strands of my hair tickle his chest. "I'm not ready to lose you in your own thoughts."

Moving my ass further down to rest on his lower legs, I trail my warm tongue down his chest, his stomach, to the fine dark hair that leads to his cock that's already coming back to life. Drawing him into my mouth, his gaze remains fixated on me, and for the next several hours, we take turns drawing out each other's pleasure until we are fully spent and satiated.

I barely recall us moving to the bed. *Did he carry me? I think I'm in a lust-induced coma.* Laying my head on his shoulder, I stare up at him, and his eyes are closed, but I know he's not sleeping because there's a faint scowl between his brows.

As if he senses me watching him, he speaks one word. "Don't."

My heart threatens to beat out of my chest, thinking what will follow that single word. Pressing my lips together, I lie quietly in his arms as he strokes his hand down my spine.

The deafening silence finally breaks in the room. "I think I'm in love with you." His voice sounds gravelly like it pained him to say it.

I've waited a lifetime for this moment, and yet the consequences of him loving me are terrifying. "Loving me is dangerous," I whisper.

"You're worth it."

I sit with my back to the headboard, drawing the sheet over my breasts, and he stays flat, placing his hand behind his head on the pillow. "I'm frightened for you, but I can't help myself. I'm in love with you, too."

He rolls to his side, peering up at me with those milk-chocolate eyes. "Are you truly done, and if so, how is your father going to handle it?"

"Not very well."

"I'll talk to him."

"No," I snap. "He can't know that I told you anything about our family." I scoot so that I'm face-to-face with him. "And until things settle down with him, he can't know about us."

"All of this is insane, but the fact of the matter is, I don't care that you're a thief. Is it wrong? Morally, yes. You've stated you're done, and that's all I need to hear. I'm not afraid of your father."

"You should be. He'll kill anyone that threatens our way of life. I think he murdered my friend." My lip quivers, thinking about Jack. "I can't let the same thing happen to you. Please promise me for now you won't mention me," I plead.

"I'm just supposed to remain his friend and act normal?" He tosses the sheets off and gets out of bed, striding naked to the bathroom as the temperature of the room that was only minutes ago heated with lust plummets, now tempered with anger.

Bolting out of bed, following him, his hands are gripped on the sink, and he's staring into the mirror. "How is this supposed to work? Secrets don't sit well with me, and lies will only build a wall between us." He exhales loudly, and his gaze shifts to mine in the mirror.

I wrap my arms around him with my chin resting on his shoulder. "I'm trying to be completely honest with you, but I can't control my father's reactions. Keeping you safe is the only thing I know to do."

"You have to promise me that life is in the past." He has a hard line between his eyes.

"I promise."

"Alright, we'll work the rest out on your terms."

"Thank you." I kiss between his shoulder blades.

"I'm going to get a quick shower. Do you want to join me?"

"Without question, but I'm dehydrated from all your sweet shenanigans, and I'm in dire need of water." I spin on my tiptoes. "I'll be back in a flash. His hand lands on my ass before I can escape out the door. I yip, and he laughs.

"Hurry back."

I can't help the smile plastered on my face. For the first time in my life, I have hope and a man I'm crazy about. Things might actually work out. Opening the fridge, I grab two bottles of water, thinking he has to be as parched as I am. *How many times did we both come? Six, seven...*my body heats up thinking about it.

A knock at the door has me scrambling, poking

my head in the bathroom. "There's someone at the door."

"It's probably just a deliveryman," he hollers.

I'm tempted to ignore it until the pounding grows firmer on the wooden door. "Persistent," I mumble, tossing my dress over my head and straightening it down my body.

"Did you need a signature or something..." I'm frozen in place when I swing the door open, and my father fills the space.

His face is expressionless, which is never good. "What the hell are you doing here?" The tone of his voice doesn't match his expression.

"I...um..." *shit, shit, shit.*

He narrows his eyes. "You and Rhett?"

I feel like a teenage girl getting caught pulling up her panties, but this is far worse. "I'm here on business. When we met at the gala, he asked if I'd go over some potential investments with him."

That seems to appease him until his gaze shifts over my shoulder, and I hear him. "Who's at the dooooor," Rhett drags out the last word.

"Do you meet all your clients wearing only a towel?" he growls and pushes me out of the way. "I'm going to kill you. We were friends, and this is how you treat me!"

I grab his arm. "This isn't what you think. Please stop!"

"What do you know?" If he had fangs, they'd be showing.

"He doesn't know anything. We're just friends." Rhett's gaze connects with mine.

"That's not true," he says, and a pit of fire grows in my stomach. "I love your daughter."

As much as I've longed for someone to profess those words to me, he has no idea what he's just done. The judge reaches behind his back where I know he carries a gun when he's not on the bench. I dart between the two of them, and he kicks the door shut with the heel of his shoe.

"Don't do this," I beg.

"He can't be brought into our lives, and you know it! How the hell did I miss this? You used our friendship to screw around with my daughter!"

"No. He had no idea until the night of the gala that you were my father."

"How long have you been seeing one another?" His jaw clenches. "He's the reason Jack lost his shit over you. He wasn't near the threat that this man is," he waves his gun around.

"Rhett isn't a threat. He loves me and wouldn't betray our secrets."

"He's betrayed our friendship, and I can't risk him exposing us."

"I'm begging you, please don't hurt him." Tears spill onto my cheeks.

"I won't tell anyone what I know because I don't want to hurt Audrey, and she's walking away from it to start another life."

"Over my dead body." He aims the gun at Rhett, and I shield him, throwing my hands in the air.

"I'll make a deal with you!" I shout.

"Now's not the time to bargain with me. Get the hell out of the way!"

"I'll give him up and keep working for you."

"No!" Rhett grinds his teeth.

"In return, he'll swear to never mention our family to anyone."

"I don't trust him."

"Then trust your own daughter."

His grip loosens on the gun. "Why should I? A few hours ago, my three daughters were willing to turn their back on everything we've built. Finley came to her senses when I threatened to have her publicly disbarred."

Bastard.

"I'll do whatever you need and pick up James's role if you'll agree to let her go."

261

Rhett spins me around to face him. "You promised me you'd stop. Don't do this. Don't let him force you into a life you no longer want. I'd rather let him kill me than have that kind of control over you."

"And I'm willing to appease you," the judge growls.

"He will kill you," I whisper, spilling tears on my dress. "I'm not going to let that happen. I promised to love the hell out of you, and this is my way of doing it." I cup his cheek. "I love you, and I will always hold a place for you in my heart."

"What's it going to be, Fox?" the judge spits.

"It's not up to him," I scream, loathing my father.

"End it with him and get your ass home. If I find out her name has so much as left your mouth, I'll return, and it won't have the same ending." He jerks the door open, tucking the gun in his belt, and stomps down the stairs.

"You're not leaving." Rhett snags me by the elbow.

I sniff, wiping the tears away with my shoulder. "I am."

He takes a step back as if I've slapped him across the face. "We can talk this out."

"There's nothing to discuss. If I don't do what he

says, you'll be a dead man. It will break my heart to walk away from us, but I can't live with you dead."

"We can leave. Go somewhere he can't find us." He's grasping for straws.

"There is no such place." I straighten my spine, putting the mask of indifference that I wear all too well in place. That hope I was feeling about my life, our life, was fleeting. The only beating heart I'll ever feel is the one I wear around my neck. It's how I've survived all these years.

I gather my bag and rub my lips together. "Forget you ever knew me."

I close the door with him staring at me, frozen in place. Shaking the emotions from my head, I mind-lessly walk down the stairs and get into my car. Rhett runs down the steps, still wearing a towel, and I peel out onto the road, nearly running over a pedestrian. My hand trembles as I unlatch the center console, finding the bottle of pills I purchased to take care of drugging Luther.

Unscrewing the cap, I tip the rim of the plastic bottle to my mouth, and several pills fall on my tongue. I swallow them dry. I don't want to feel the pain that's sharp enough to cut my heart and heavy enough to drown me. I drive fast and furious down Ocean Drive with no destination in mind. The curves wind around the shoreline, and I pass cars at a high rate of speed. As the drugs start to take effect, numbness eases in my veins, carrying away the pain. The feeling that I can fly takes hold of me, and my foot grows heavier and heavier on the pedal. My eyes blur as the road turns sharp.

A tractor trailer swerves, laying on its horn, barely missing me. I don't let up my speed when I see flashing lights behind me. "You want me, come and get me!" My engine screams, hitting a hundred and forty miles an hour.

The road curves again, and taillights are in front of me. Slamming on the brakes, my car spins and spins. I see the world upside down and hear the crunching of metal before everything goes dark.

Chapter 23
♥AUDREY

"AUDREY, CAN YOU HEAR ME?"

A bright light shines in my eye with someone tugging at my eyelid.

"Audrey," the woman's voice sounds familiar, but there's so much ringing in my ears I can't make it out.

"Start another bag of saline and call the orthopedic surgeon."

James. It's James. My eyelids flutter as I try to open them.

"Audrey, you're in the emergency room."

"James," I rasp. "What happened?" I rub my aching forehead.

"You wrecked your car, and you're lucky to be in one piece."

"My arm hurts," I wince.

"It's broken, and maybe a few ribs."

"I don't remember."

"Can I have a minute alone with my sister," she says, and everyone leaves the room.

"You're high, aren't you?" She has squatted down and is next to my ear. "I thought you'd given up the drugs."

"I did." I swallow hard as Rhett's face flashes in my mind.

"What happened?"

"The judge." A bubble of a cry leaps from my throat. "I was with Rhett, and he caught us. He threatened him with a gun and said he'd kill him if I didn't walk away and dared Rhett to ever speak our name again."

"Damn him," she snarls. "You're going back to our bloodline of work, aren't you?"

"What choice do I have?"

"I hate him."

"You're free. I promised if he'd let Rhett live and let you go, I'd do whatever he wanted."

"You shouldn't have done that. I was leaving anyway."

"He wouldn't have let you. He told Finley he'd have her disbarred if she didn't drop the notion of bailing on our family antics. I have no doubt he'd have your medical license pulled."

She kicks over a metal tray, sending it crashing across the floor. "Damn him to hell!"

I clutch my arm to my side and grimace through the pain when I sit on the edge of the gurney.

"Don't get up." She lays her hands on my shoulders and guides me back down gently. "I have a surgeon coming to look at your X-rays."

"I'm fine. I need to get out of here."

"You can't. There are cops waiting outside to take you to jail. I'll make sure they don't get their hands on your drug test, but I can't do anything about the reckless driving warrant."

"I'd rather be in jail than go home." My eyes fill with tears. "I love him, and I can't have him."

"I'm so sorry, Audrey." She sweeps hair off my forehead. "I hate this for you."

"Please just give me something for the pain," I sob. She knows it's for the pain in my chest and not my arm.

"Okay." She draws up liquid into a syringe and pushes it into my IV, and as soon as it flows through my veins, I close my eyes, letting it roll over me like the waves in the ocean, with the tide pulling me deeper into the blue water. I can taste the salty water and feel the heat warming my face. Stretching my arms wide, I float. Staring up at the sky, snippets of my life come together, followed by a deep-seated pain.

The mother I never knew.

The kind, gentle father I can't remember.

My sisters' heartaches.

The love I'll never have.

The riptide pulls me under, and I don't fight it. Barely able to keep my head above water, I give in, not wanting to face the life ahead of me.

* * *

"She's waking up." Finley's voice is close by, and someone squeezes my hand.

"You're out of surgery." James's voice pulls me out of the darkness.

"My arm," I rasp, my throat as dry as the Sahara desert.

"The surgeon had to put it back together with plates and several pins, but you'll make a full recovery."

I open my eyes, and my vision is blurry at first, and then I suck in air when I see my father standing at the foot of my bed with his hands resting on the footboard.

"Get out." In my mind, I yelled, but the words hardly come out.

"You had me worried." He stands tall.

"This is your fault."

"I didn't force a few pills down your throat. That's on you."

James gets to her feet. "You should leave," she snarls.

"Whether any of you believe it or not, I love you."

"You have a funny way of showing it." Finley crosses her arms over her chest.

"I only want to protect you."

"We're the ones that need protecting from you." James moves next to him. "You threaten Finley's livelihood, and then you wave a gun at the man Audrey loves. If that's your sick version of love, then I don't want anything to do with it."

"It's for her own good. We can't risk an outsider in our lives. This is not news to any of you."

"What's to stop us from exposing you?" James is treading on dangerous territory.

"You'll take yourselves down if you do, and"—he waves a finger—"I'm not going to let that happen. The three of you agreed to this a long time ago, and don't kid yourselves into thinking you haven't enjoyed the hunt. You have my blood running through you, and you need this as much as I need to breathe."

269

"We have our mother in us too." James clasps her charm. "She'd hate this and you."

His face hardens, and he clenches his teeth. "Don't you ever say that to me again."

His look is so fierce that James backs away.

I reach out and touch her arm. "It doesn't matter. You're free of him now."

"But the two of you aren't." Her gaze sweeps between me and Finley.

"He's right," Finley says, blowing out a long breath. "I don't like his threat, but his words are truthful. Making people pay for their wrongdoings is the reason I love being an attorney, so playing Robin Hood, I have to admit, comes with a lot of satisfaction that I can't get from the court system. I agreed to leave to support you, and now I don't have to. Audrey made a deal for your freedom."

"At what cost to her? Giving up the only man she's ever cared about? He gets to know what it feels like to love, but she doesn't?" Her voice fills the room.

He exhales. "I'm honestly sorry, but it has to be this way."

"I've got patients to see." James storms by him.

"Wait. I need to get out of here."

All sets of eyes swing to mine. "The cops are

going to haul you in as soon as you're released." Finley strokes my arm.

"You need to take care of this." I grind my teeth, glaring at the judge.

"I'm afraid I can't this time."

"Can't or won't?" I hiss.

"You'll spend the night in jail, and I'll bail you out tomorrow. Besides, a night behind bars might do you some good, along with some rehab." He follows James out of the room.

"I'll see what I can do," Finley says. "Rehab isn't a bad idea. You could have died."

"In the moment, I didn't care."

"Even if you don't, I do."

I rest my head on the pillow. "What's done is done. Rhett's out of my life. Our father wins. Jack's dead, and..." My lip quivers.

"You'll always have me and James." She sits next to me, gently cradling me in her arms like a mother would. "I love you."

"I love you, too." My tears fall on her shoulders until there are no more.

"I'm going to make a few phone calls to the chief of police." She gets to her feet.

"Thank you for always being here for me."

"It's what sisters do."

James enters as Finley is leaving. "Do you need anything?"

"Something for pain would be nice."

She sits on the edge of the bed. "Promise me you won't take any more pills."

"I'd like to swear to you that I won't, but it's the only thing that eases the ache inside of me."

"I understand that feeling well." Her eyes are holding a secret.

"What haven't you told me?"

She presses her lips together like she's debating whether or not to say anything.

"You know you can share anything with me."

"I was in love with Jack," she whispers her admission.

My heart falls to the floor, and I'm in disbelief. "What? Why didn't you ever say anything?"

"Because he didn't love me."

"Why didn't I see it and how?"

"When you'd send him on his way, swearing it would be the last time every time, he'd come crying to me. We became friends. At least, that's what he felt."

"Oh, James. I'm so sorry. I wish you would have told me." I cling to her with a hug.

"It didn't matter. He didn't love me, and me

telling you or him wouldn't have changed that." She pauses. "He's gone." I feel her tears on my cheek.

"I wish I would have known."

"Do you really think our father killed him?" She leans back to look me in the eye.

"I don't know, but I don't believe Jack was the type of person to take his own life."

"I don't either," she sniffs.

"The thought of what our father is capable of and seeing him wield a gun on Rhett is the sole reason I agreed to give him up."

"You traded your freedom for mine."

"You and Finley gave up your childhood to take care of me. There isn't anything I wouldn't do for you."

"Then you'll stop with the drugs. I can't bear the thought of my baby sister not being around anymore, and you came too close this time."

"Alright."

"Rehab?"

"Yes," I agree.

The door swings open. "The cops have been called off. You'll pay a fine, and your license will be suspended, but you won't be spending the night in jail," Finley says.

"Thank you." I lie back, the weight of the day hitting me like a ton of bricks, and I feel so tired.

"I'll make sure you get a little something for pain so you can sleep." James stands.

"I really am sorry," I say softly, and she leaves the room.

"She finally told you, didn't she?"

"You knew how she felt about Jack?" I scowl. "Why didn't you tell me?"

"She asked me not to."

"I feel so guilty for the way I treated him, even more so now. James should hate me."

"She doesn't hate you. In a way, she understood your need for him, being he's the only person the judge would let near you. James knew he didn't return her feelings."

"It doesn't make it any easier to swallow."

"No, but perhaps, with drugs out of your system, you'll think about how your actions affect other people."

She's right. I'm to blame for it all. "How am I just supposed to step back in line with our chaotic lives?"

"I know it's hard to believe sometimes, but in his own delusional way, our father loves us and wants to protect his daughters."

. . .

I need you to love him no matter what. Don't desert him. Coax him back to the light with love and understanding. Be firm, and never be scared to tell him how you feel.

The realization hits me hard how much he needs us, and I sink against the bed, closing my eyes. "I'm so tired."

"Get some rest. I'll come back tomorrow and take you home."

Chapter 24
♥ RHETT

I'M LOSING my damn mind. I've texted Audrey multiple times over the past two weeks with no response. Her phone goes straight to voicemail, and I haven't seen her car drive by the coffee shop. I keep thinking she'll change her mind and we'll find a way to be together. My heart is broken, and I'm not sure how to deal with it. It's not something I've had to reckon with in my life.

When I joined the military, I left behind my high school sweetheart. We had grown in different directions, and I knew if I stayed, we'd eventually go our separate ways, so leaving ended something sooner I knew would never last. But Audrey...from the moment I saw her at the bar...I wanted her...needed her.

Two days after she left, I received a delivery at my apartment with a handwritten note from her.

Please open immediately is all it said until I looked inside and found a fifteen-pound cat and another envelope.

"Shambles." I picked her up, setting her on my lap. "What the hell?"

I reached inside and took out the note.

Rhett,

Shambles deserves a better life than living with my messed-up family. She liked you the minute you touched her, just like her owner did. Please take good care of her. She's sweet, yet sometimes stubborn, again like her owner. My life is in shambles, and hers doesn't have to be. I'm giving you a piece of me by asking you to love her.

I'm sorry I got you involved in my life, but I don't regret one minute of the time we spent together. You gave me more love and hope than I've ever felt. Please forgive me for walking away, but know that I did it to keep you safe. I'm not blameless in my life choices, and if I'm being totally honest with you, part of me feeds off of it. Righting wrongs, feeling like I'm making a difference in someone else's misfortune. Paying a sentence for the loss of my mother. What I'm trying to clear up is, that even though I said I'd turn my back on it, deep down, I know it was a lie, and lies come way too easy for me. But, I never lied to you about how I felt when I was in your arms. It's the one truth in my life that's burned into my heart.

I WILL NEVER FORGET YOU!
This is me loving you enough and letting go,
Audrey

PS. Take care of Shambles. You need to know how much she likes pasta. She will turn into a bug-eyed, demonic-looking creature and fight you for it. Don't say you weren't warned.

I know every word was sincere because of the tear stains on the letter. Shambles curled in my lap like she belonged, and she's taken over my comforter every night since. The part about the pasta was not an exaggeration. I made spaghetti, and as soon as it hit the strainer, Shambles jumped up in the sink and ran off with a mouthful of it. I found it in various places all over the apartment, like a squirrel hiding nuts for the winter.

Every morning, I find her perched in the window like she's looking for Audrey. I join her, hoping to see her, while Shambles arches her back, purring, wanting attention.

"She thinks she knows what's best for both of us," I tell her, but she's wrong. We both need her."

I glance at my watch, knowing I've lingered as long as I can. "There's a big hockey tournament today," I tell the cat like she's interested in my life.

"I gotta go. I'll bring you back a treat."

Shambles meows.

"I know, pasta." I chuckle.

Grabbing my gear, I hustle down the stairs and shake thoughts of Audrey out of my head. I have to focus on the game. The boys are so excited, and they've hit the ice hard all week, wanting to beat the team they've lost to twice.

The boys are anxiously early and waiting for me in the locker room. They are all gathered together, but Nelly who is sitting on a bench near his locker with his head hanging downward.

"What's up with him?" I ask Charlie.

"I don't know. He hasn't spoken since his mom dropped him off."

"Take the team to the ice and start warmups," I tell him, and they follow him out.

I sit on the bench beside Nelly. "Are you okay?"

He doesn't say anything.

I slide my hand to his shoulder. "You can talk to me."

"My dad didn't come home last night," he says as a tear drops on the locker room floor.

"Sometimes parents fight."

"It's not that." He peers up at me. "Mom said he was upset that his business deals didn't go through, and she mumbled something about his partner cheating him out of the deal. She dropped me off to go look for him. I'm really worried."

"The backup goalie can play. I'll call your mom and have her pick you up."

"No. She doesn't want me to miss out on this game. She promised she'd find him and everything would be alright."

"How about this? When the game is over, we'll both go help look for him if she's not located him by then."

He sits tall, sniffs, and wipes his nose with the back of his hand. "I'd like that. Thank you."

I ruffle his mop of hair. "Get out there and do your best, and if at any time you change your mind, let me know and we'll make the change."

He stands. "I'm doing this for my dad. I'm going to make him proud of me."

I get to my feet. "He's already proud of you. Get your gear and get on the ice."

He grabs his helmet and water bottle and picks

up his feet so his blades don't scrap across the concrete floor.

I tuck in my shirt tail and pull down the sleeves of my sports jacket, following him into the ice arena and finding my spot behind the bench. The other team is on the ice warming up, too, and the countdown clock to the game has already started.

Parents and families have filled the bleachers. I scan them quickly for Audrey, but there's no sign of her. I let the ache inside me go and focus on the boys. The buzzer sounds, and the team gathers at the bench with all eyes on me.

"You guys got this. Each of you is good at your position. Don't let them get in your head. Play your game. You're champions. Do it honorably."

Nelly nods and skates to the net with his game face on. The other players take their positions. Fila-pose readies himself for the face-off. The referee drops the puck, and Filapose fights for it, sending it to Lefty.

From that point on, they dominated the game. The other team played rough, checking our players and earning several penalties, giving us the advantage with power plays.

Nelly shut them out, not allowing one puck past

him. He's fearless and quick, playing like he doesn't have a heavy weight on his shoulders.

Several times after we broke from time outs, I'd look into the bleachers because I could swear I felt Audrey's presence, but it was just my imagination, longing for a woman I can't have.

The last buzzer sounds, and the boys raise their sticks in the air and huddle in the middle of the ice, cheering. The score is 4-0. One by one, they line up, bumping their gloves with the opposing team.

I walk over to the other bench and shake the coach's hand.

"You've done a remarkable job with those boys," he says, and I swim with pride.

I meet the players back in the locker room, and they are all hyped up, except for Nelly. The worry is back on his face, and he's carrying it on his shoulders.

"I'm so stinking proud of all of you. You've worked hard, and you deserved this win!"

"Thanks to you, Coach," Willie hails.

"This is all on you guys. Each of you has the talent. I just guided it."

Nelly has already removed his uniform and is tying his Converse shoes. "Are we still going, Coach?"

"You bet. Let me call your mother first and find out where we can help look." I step outside of the building and find a quiet spot, dialing Mary's number.

Her voice cracks when she answers the phone. "Hello."

"Hey, this is Coach Fox. The game is over, and the boys won. Nelly played amazingly. He told me about his father, and I offered to help look for him after the game."

"I found him," she says, through a sob.

"Is he alright?"

"He's on life support at the hospital."

I run my hand through my hair. "Shit."

"The police found him laying face down in a hotel room. He..." she stammers, "tried to kill himself."

"I'm so sorry. What do you want me to tell Nelly?" My heart aches for the kid.

"Can you bring him to the hospital?"

"Yes, absolutely."

"Don't give him any details other than he's alive. Tell him he was in an accident, and I'll explain it to him when he's here."

"Alright. We'll be there within thirty minutes." I hang up. How do you explain to a kid that your father wanted to end his life? I don't envy any of them.

Nelly is outside the ice rink, rolling his bag behind him. "Did she find him?"

"Yes. I'm going to take you to them."

"Thank God." His tense shoulders relax. "Is he at home?"

I brace my hand on the back of his neck. "They are at the hospital. Your mom said she'd explain everything when I bring you to her."

The tension returns, coiling in his shoulders. "Is he alive?"

"Yes." It's not a lie.

"Okay then," he says. "Take me to him."

Traffic is brutal, but the Uber driver weaves his way to the front of the hospital. Nelly has literally been bouncing in the seat next to me with uneasiness permeating from his body. As soon as the driver stops, he hops out, running for the entrance. I grab his bag and catch up with him.

Mary texted me on the way with his room number. They are on the third floor. He reaches the elevator and pushes the button, then rocks back and forth on his heels as if he's willing it to hurry up.

"I'm going to take the stairs," he says, and I snag his arm when the elevator door pings.

He pushes the number three button several times, and I wrap my arm around his shoulder. "Easy."

We stop at a set of double doors.

"He's in ICU?" he chokes out.

"I'll get us buzzed in," I say, pressing a button.

A voice comes over a small black box, asking who we are here to see. I tell her, and the doors ding, opening.

Nelly bolts inside as soon as they are wide enough to push through. The room number is straight in front of us, and Mary sees Nelly through the glass windows surrounding her husband's room. He runs into her arms, and she thanks me with puffy, bloodshot eyes.

I don't enter the room, but stay close by. Nelly cries and leans over his father's bed, hugging him.

Mary steps outside the small room, giving Nelly time with his dad.

"Thank you for caring about my son."

"He's a good kid. Is there anything I can do for you?"

She shakes her head. "I just don't understand why he'd do this." She sobs on my shoulder. "He couldn't handle disappointing us. The cops found a letter. He lost every dime we saved in his project. The money is all gone. His partner cut him out of their deal and ran off with the investment money. He was so ashamed." She whips her head up. "I didn't care about the money. It's not worth his life, but if I ever get my hands on his partner, I just might strangle him with my own hands," she cries in anger. "Does that make me a bad person?"

"No. Not at all." For the first time, I truly understand why Audrey finds some sort of satisfaction in what she does. I don't know the man, and I want to make him pay for the pain he's caused this family.

"I don't know what I'm going to do if he doesn't pull through. Nelly won't ever understand. It will change him, and he's come so far."

It changed Benjamin Steel to lose his wife, blaming others. "Can you tell me anything about his partner?"

"I have his name, but that's it. The police said the address they had on file for him is bogus. What are we going to do?" She continues to cry, and the warmth of her tears wet my jacket.

"I think I know someone who can help."

"Really?" She blinks, looking up at me.

"Text me his name."

"Okay." She swallows.

"Keep me updated on the situation here, and if you need a place for Nelly to stay, he's welcome to my place. I'm going to step in and tell him bye."

She nods, sniffing.

I lay the palm of my hand on the flat of his back, feeling the pain inside of him trembling. "He's going to be okay." I pray it's not a lie. "I'm a phone call away if you need me. You're welcome to stay at my place."

"I'm not leaving his side or my mother's," he bawls.

There's nothing more for me to say to him. Seeing his father's face and the tubes coming out of his body keeping him alive, I'm filled with rage for Nelly and his mom. My jaw clenches as I storm out of his room, wanting to make things right for this kid.

Chapter 25
♥ AUDREY

"LORD HE'S beautiful in that suit," I whisper to myself. This hideous wig itches like hell, and I look ridiculous. James helped me get dressed since my arm is in a cast and fastened the sling around my shoulder. I had to lie to her, being that it's Saturday and the office is closed. I told her I was behind on work, and she dropped me off at my office. I didn't tell her about the hockey game today. She's headed back home to pack, finally moving out. She's hung around the past two weeks to help me out. I'm truly going to miss having her around, but I'm happy she's free.

The judge has given her a hard time and has tried every tactic, including trying to play on her pity. She's stood her ground with him, but it hasn't backed him off.

She's been teaching me how to break into safes, and it's been difficult with only one hand in use, but she's a good teacher, and I finally got the hang of it. I asked her if she was going to miss it?

"I will miss being in this house with you and Finley," was her response.

There's never been a time the three of us haven't been together, and our home will seem empty without her in it. I'm envious of her fresh start, and I long to hold Rhett.

He texted me so many times, and it was everything I could do to keep from responding. I changed my phone number to keep him safe. I know the judge; he'll be checking to see if we've kept our word and stayed apart. I exited the back of my building and took two cabs to get here, making sure I wasn't followed because it's not beyond him to hire someone to watch my every move.

Rhett looks good, but his pain shows in his eyes even from this distance. His gaze skims the bleachers, and my heart thumps hard, knowing he's searching for me in the crowd. "I'm here," I say softly. I've missed him with every fiber of my being. My head knows I'm doing what's best for him, but my chest is in a constant state of ache, and I've sworn off drugs to ease my pain. No drugs, no sex— my life is crap. I don't even have Shambles to complain to. Giving her to Rhett was me giving him a piece of me, but I miss her complaining too. Rhett has broken me from wanting to have sex with any other man. Celibacy is the consequence of the things I've done.

The game starts, and I'm on the edge of my seat, cheering for the Sharks, for Rhett. They look even stronger than the last time I saw them play. The other team checks Charlie hard, and I cringe at the impact. He shakes it off and gets the puck back, scoring with a shot from behind his back as if to say *F* you to the opposing team.

Nelly is on point with every single puck flying toward the goal. He's a lot of fun to watch. It's odd, though. He's not smiling like he normally does.

Charlie takes another hard hit, then Santiago and Willie flank the player that crushed him into the wall, and they hit him at the same time. His helmet flies off, and he smacks hard on the ice. A fight erupts, but no penalty is called on the Sharks. They look so good on the ice, and Rhett is beaming with pride when the last period ends. I slip out with the crowd unnoticed and call Finley for a ride home.

As soon as my arm is healed, I'm purchasing another car, maybe one a tad bit tamer that doesn't stand out as much.

Finley cruises up, and I hop in the passenger side.

"Are you up for a drink?" she asks as I shake my hair free of the wig.

"What did you have in mind?"

"A frozen mango margarita at the beach club. It's a beautiful evening, and the sun will be setting soon."

"Why not? I have nothing better to do." I sigh.

"You're torturing yourself and risking getting caught sneaking to watch the hockey game."

"It was an important one for the boys, and I wanted to be there. This town isn't so big that the judge can't expect me not to run into Rhett. I miss him." I exhale loudly.

"I'm sorry you had to sacrifice him for our family." She weaves in and out of traffic until she makes the turn into the parking lot of the outside bar. Finley orders drinks for the two of us, and I find a small table out on the sand.

When she finds me carrying our drinks, she sets them on the table and then lowers her sunglasses a smidge. "Get a load of the two hot bodies tossing the football."

"A little young for you, don't you think?"

"I'm not looking to marry them. A hard body and a good roll in the sack might lighten both our moods."

"I'm not interested." I suck through the straw and instantly regret the brain freeze.

"Suit yourself." She removes her sunglasses and her cover-up to reveal a tiny white bikini, then tosses her things in her bag.

"How am I supposed to get home?"

"Either call James or a cab." She starts to walk off and looks over her shoulder. "Not Rhett!"

"Not Rhett," I mimic like a petulant child.

"Good to see you're on the mend." I hear a familiar voice behind me.

"Colin," I speak his name when he joins me at the table.

"When are you coming back to the office?"

"I'm good, thank you," I snark and press the sugary rim to my lips. "Do you ever talk about anything but work?"

He drums his fingers on the steel table. "You're right. How are you doing?"

"Honestly, pretty shitty."

"Do you want to talk about it?"

"I met someone, fell in love, and it's over," I state flatly, staring at him.

"Audrey Steel let someone close to that frozen heart?" He half laughs.

"Why did I bother telling you anything?" I roll my eyes.

"I'm sorry, it's just that you're always so well put together, and I've never seen you take a personal stance with anyone. You've shot me down a million times."

"A million and one." I smirk.

"I am curious. What kind of man got your attention?"

"A sweet, gentle, caring, closed-off man who let me in."

"Not at all the type I picture you falling for."

"Let me guess. You think my perfect man would be exceedingly wealthy, own lots of properties all over the world, arrogant, and has one of the most expensive cars in the world."

"That pretty much sums it up."

"He was none of those things," I rasp, biting the inside corner of my lip.

"Your looks lie. There is more to you than a strong, successful businesswoman with a cold heart. I never pictured you having a soft spot, but you do."

"Let's keep that secret between the two of us. It might not bode well for my line of work."

"May I buy you another drink?" He tilts his chin toward my almost empty glass.

"Thanks, but it doesn't mean you and I are cozying up."

"Got it. I truly am sorry that you got hurt."

"I'll bounce back."

"I have no doubt about that. You're Audrey Steel, the smartest and savviest businesswoman I know. You could snap your fingers, and men would be bowing at your feet." He smiles and kicks the sand as he makes his way to the bar.

"There's only one man I want," I say, polishing off my margarita.

Colin buys three more rounds and pays to have extra tequila shots floating on top of them. I'm undoubtedly feeling no pain. Finley disappeared and texted me an hour later that she wouldn't be coming home tonight. Colin offered me a ride, but he's as tipsy as I am, so I settle on an Uber.

Walking in the front door, my father is sitting on the couch, reading a magazine. "Where have you been?"

"None of your business," I slur boldly.

"Another client has fallen in my lap."

"Good for you," I snap.

"You're going to have to lose this attitude with me." He raises an eyebrow.

"Not tonight I don't. Tomorrow is a new day."

"I'll expect you to be cooperative."

I wave my middle finger at him once I've walked past his view.

Stripping out of my clothes, I sink on the bed, lying on the top of the comforter. It's lonely in here without Shambles," I mumble and close my eyes.

I lift my head when I hear my door slide open. "James," I say.

"Hey." She lies next to me. "I'm all packed."

"Are you leaving tonight?" I roll to my side, tucking my hand under my cheek.

"No. I'll wait until morning." She peers around the bedroom. "Where is that feral cat of yours?"

"She deserved a better life than with me, so I gave her to Rhett."

"I'm so sorry the two of you can't have a life together."

"Me too." A single tear slips from the corner of my eye. "Life goes on, right? The judge already has another job lined up for us. At least it will keep me busy and my mind off of Rhett."

She kisses my forehead. "Get some sleep. I promised the judge I wouldn't leave until after dinner tomorrow night. I think he believes he can still convince me to stay."

"He can believe what he wants. We'll consider it

one last dinner before your freedom to live the life you want."

"I love you, Audrey," she says from the doorway.

"Love you too. Good night."

* * *

Sunday starts way too early, and I'm in dire need of ibuprofen and a strong pot of coffee. The judge is sitting at the table with his hands cupped around a mug.

"Is there any of that left?" I ask, motioning toward his cup.

"Fresh pot."

"Finley just slinked in the door about an hour ago. She looked like she had been up all night."

"Good for her," I mumble, pouring the hot liquid into my favorite mug.

"You and I need to call a truce." He scoots the chair out next to him with his foot, offering me a seat.

I squint and take the one on the opposite side of the table. "Does this truce allow me to be in Rhett's life?"

"No. And believe it or not, I'm sorry about it. I

truly liked him. I think he's a good man, which is why he doesn't belong in our world."

I genuinely believe he's sorry by the way his eyes soften, staring at me.

"The choices I've made for our family have cost each of you girls sorely. If your mother were still alive..." his voice trails off.

"You'd be a different man."

He nods.

"We can stop."

"This thing has a hook in me that I can't let go of. I need you and your sisters to make it work."

"And we need our own lives separate from all the chaos."

"We're criminals in the eyes of the law. None of us can detach ourselves from what we do. It would only cause heartache in others that we are close to, and I can't ask, nor will I have others become like us. Can't you see I'm only trying to protect you?"

"That doesn't make any of this any easier."

He puts his mug down and folds his hands together, leaning on his elbows. "Do you want to hear about the case that fell in my lap?"

"What else do I have to do. You've effectively squelched me having a love life."

"We are going to take down the owners of a franchise of nursing homes."

There is no one lower than someone taking advantage of the elderly. "I'm listening."

"I knew this one would be right up your alley." He smiles, and the conversation goes on for several hours.

When he's done, I stand. "I'm going for a walk."

"I'll expect you for dinner this evening. James will be leaving afterward."

Chapter 26
♥ RHETT

I'VE WORN a path from my place to the hospital in the past twenty-four hours, making sure Nelly and his mom have everything they need. Nelly called me around lunchtime to tell me his father had awoken from his coma but wasn't speaking. I asked him to put his mother on the phone, and she spoke in soft sobs of relief that he was going to live. The doctors said only time would tell what, if any, deficits he might have, but it would be a long recovery for him and his family. She didn't know how they were going to pay for any of it.

"Don't worry about the money," I assured her. I had already put the word out among the other hockey team members' families, and donations were already starting to come in, yet I knew it would never be enough for them to recover.

Doing a deep dive into the Steel family, I finally gain access to their address via Ben's golf club membership. "Wish me luck." I scratch Shambles's back, and she arches into my hand, meowing. "I put out a bowl of pasta on the counter. Help yourself." As if she understands me, she leaps on the counter and feasts on the long strands of noodles.

"If I don't make it back, I'm sure Audrey will rescue you."

Once I'm on the sidewalk, I hail a cab and give the driver my destination. He makes the turn onto Ocean Drive, and my chest begins to ache, not only at the thought of seeing Audrey but that Ben may put a bullet through my chest for showing up at their door.

"Don't pull into the driveway. Just drop me off at the entrance," I direct him, handing him cash.

Walking the long palm-lined driveway has my heart racing with each step closer to the mansion residing at the end of the drive. "I have to do this for Nelly," I inhale sharply.

Before I make it to the door, I see a camera sweeping in my direction. I know they know I'm here and fully expect the door to swing open any second.

As I make it to the steps, Audrey bolts out, running toward me, planting her hand in the middle of my chest. "You can't be here," she says with her eyes wide with fear.

"What the hell happened to you? Did he do

this?" My teeth grind, seeing her arm in a cast and a deep purple bruise on the side of her face.

"No. I totaled my car."

"I need to talk to your father."

She peers over her shoulder and sees Ben gripping a pistol barreling out of the garage door.

"I told you I never wanted to see you again!" she yells.

"This isn't about us." I take a step back, holding my hands wide to my sides with my palms up.

"Get the hell off of my property before I shoot you for trespassing." Ben's gun is now aimed at me. "You're lucky I'm even giving you a warning."

Audrey steps between us. "Don't! He's leaving, and he won't be back."

"I need your help." I sidestep her.

"I don't believe there is anything I can do for you." He cocks his head to the side.

"I need your services, or whatever it is you call it. I have a friend who's been betrayed by a partner and took every dime he had."

Audrey tugs at my arm. "You don't know what you're asking."

Gently placing my hands on her forearms, I square my body with hers. "I understand why you and your family do the things that you do, and I want in on it."

Her gaze rocks back and forth with mine. "What happened?"

I twist my neck to look at Ben. "If he'll let me inside, I'll tell you."

Ben's jaw visibly locks. "If I let you in my house, and I don't believe you, they'll never find your body."

I swallow hard. "Understood."

He tucks the gun in the back of his pants and waves me inside the house.

"Please don't do this. I'm begging you," Audrey says softly.

I lift my hand, placing it on the side of her face. "You need to know I love you, but this isn't about you. It's about Nelly and his family."

Her eyes narrow. "Nelly?"

"Yes, and the Steel family is the only way I know to help him, even if it costs me my life."

She takes my hand in hers and leads me through her house to the dining area where Finley and James are sitting with Ben standing at the end of the table.

"You have exactly ten minutes to convince me I shouldn't kill you." Ben crosses his arms over his chest.

I sit, and Audrey takes the chair closest to me. "What happened to Nelly?" she asks.

"Edward Nelson invested his entire savings and remortgaged his home on an investment he went into with a business associate. For the sake of time" —I lock my gaze with Ben—"the business partner stole the money and left town. Nelly's dad couldn't face his family, so he went to a hotel room and shot himself."

Audrey gasps. "No!"

"He's lucky to be alive."

"Oh, thank God." She exhales, clutching my hand.

"Now they are faced with losing their home and can't afford the care he's going to need."

"Son of a bitch!" Ben slams his fists on the table.

"Do you have any information on the partner?" Finley asks.

I pull out a piece of paper from my jeans pocket and slide it across the table to her. "This is all I know. The police found the address he had listed to be phony."

"I'm betting money his name is an alias." Finley disappears for a moment and returns with a laptop.

"I didn't say we were going to help him," Ben snaps.

"Why wouldn't we? This is right up our alley." Finley taps the keyboard.

"I'm going to help him regardless if you do or not." Audrey stares him down.

"Me too," James pipes in.

Audrey's head whips toward her sisters. "No. You're out of here today. You have a life waiting for you."

"One last job," she says sternly.

"We have a customer already lined up," Ben adds.

"They can wait," Finley interjects and turns the laptop toward me. "Just as I thought, an alias. Seems he's not new to this game."

"How the hell did you do that so quickly?"

"We're professionals." Ben sticks his chin in the air.

"I'm in," Finley states.

"If we do this, you'll walk away from this family and move out of town." Ben glares at me.

I get to my feet. "No. I love your daughter, and I'm not going anywhere. Your Robin Hood tendencies don't scare me, and I want in on every part of it. I would never betray your daughter or any of you."

Audrey stands, wrapping her arms around my waist. "God, I love you."

"So what's it going to be. Am I leaving here with my body rolled up in a carpet, or are you going to help me and accept the fact that I'm going to be part of this messed-up family?"

Ben's chest rises with a deep inhale, and he slowly strides in front of me. His tongue is clenched between his teeth, while his right hand is fisted at his side. I steady myself to be punched in the gut or the face, and I'm surprised when he holds out his hand.

"Welcome to the family."

I shake his hand firmly. "Thank you."

"This doesn't mean I won't keep my eye on you, and I reserve the right to still take you out."

"I understand."

He angles his head at Finley. "Find the details. I'll call our other client and tell them there's been a minor delay." He marches out of the dining room with his phone already pressed to his ear.

Audrey clasps my hand and drags me through the house to what I assume is her bedroom and throws her body against mine once she's shut us inside. "I can't believe you did that." Her mouth crashes with mine. "I was so scared when I saw you walking up our driveway."

"I was too," I say against her lips. "I've missed you so damn much."

Our mouths unlock, and she buries her head on my chest. "I didn't want to give you up. You know I did it to keep you safe."

"Yes, but it still hurt like hell."

"I'm sorry."

"No more lies, Audrey. Not to me." I inch back and lay both of my hands on either side of her face, forcing her to look at me.

"I promise."

"We are in this together from now on."

"I was at the tournament."

"I didn't see you."

"I wore a hideous wig," she scrunches her nose. "I had to see you. The boys were amazing." She takes a step back from me. "Wait, I remember thinking Nelly looked sad."

"His dad was missing at that point, and his mother convinced him to play. It wasn't until after the game he found out that his father attempted suicide."

"Poor kid." Tears fill her eyes. "Is there anything I can do for him?"

"We," I emphasize the word *we*, "are going to help him by the Steel method."

"Are you one hundred percent sure you want to be involved? We can handle this on our own, and you can walk away."

"That's not an option. I won't walk away from any of this. I've never felt such rage and heartache for a family in my life. I understood completely how it must make you feel to make people pay for harming others purposely for crimes they get away with."

She walks in a circle. "You have to understand there's no going back."

"I don't want to, especially if it means I get to spend my life with you."

"The judge will be watching your every move."

"Let him. I won't give him a reason not to trust me."

She folds her body in my arms. "I can't believe this is happening. I never thought I'd find someone who would accept me or my family."

"It's part of loving you, Audrey. All of you. Not just the outward appearance. It's the woman on the inside I fell madly in love with."

"So you're saying if I was hideously ugly, you'd still love me?"

"Absolutely." I tilt her chin and kiss her sweetly.

"Liar." She chuckles, leaning into the kiss.

"Shambles misses you, and I've had to take stock in pasta." I grin against her lips.

"We can discuss Shambles later. All I want right now is you buried deep inside of me."

"You never have to ask." I pick her up, laying her on the bed. "What about your arm?"

She unclasps the sling. "I'm pretty sure I can do this one-handed."

Chapter 27
♥AUDREY

"FAMILY MEETING!" Finley pounds on my bedroom door at seven in the morning.

Rhett runs his hand down his face, trying to wake up, being that we didn't fall asleep until the wee hours of the morning. It felt so good being in his arms, but part of me is still afraid for him. Does he really know what he's getting himself into and the risks he'll be taking with his freedom?

His hand finds my hip and squeezes. "Stop worrying about me. I can see it in the corners of your eyes. I know what I want, and that's you."

"I come with lots of baggage."

"So do I."

"Are you coming or not!" Finley yells.

"I guess we better get up." He chuckles.

"I love you, and I want to tell you every day."

"And I want to hear it," he says, tossing the sheets off of him and tugging his jeans over his hips.

I get up and throw on a pair of shorts and a tank

309

top, twisting my hair into a bun the best I can using one hand.

"I like that look on you." He winks with a smirk.

"Well, the bare feet on you does it for me." I laugh, and we walk out of the bedroom, holding hands.

James has mugs filled with coffee, handing them to each of us. The judge is already at the head of the table waiting on us. Finley has her reading glasses on and files laid out at the table.

"Did you get any sleep," I ask, squeezing her shoulder.

"You know me, I'm like a dog with a bone when I need to be."

The judge is glaring at Rhett. "Morning," he grunts.

"James, I'm sad to see you here this morning." I hug her.

"It's only a temporary delay in my plans. You're my sister, and I want to help."

"Fredrick Kinsley is his real name. He's resided in ten different states and set up fake investment companies in each of them, leaving with his victim's life savings. He's a smooth-talking conman. He's been good at evading the authorities, but I've found him."

Our father sets his mug down. "Mr. Kinsley has a cabin hidden in the mountains of North Carolina. James has already tracked his credit card to the area."

"You guys work fast," Rhett states.

"Some of us were up all night working, not messing around." He scowls.

I get up and open a drawer in a cabinet where we keep maps of every state and locate the one I need, spreading it on the table. Finley points to the location. "This is where he'll be hiding. After his misdeeds, he returns to his safe haven for two months and then moves to his next victim. That's his pattern."

"When we're done with him, the place will be torched. There will be no place for him to hide," I circle the area with a red pen on the map.

"I'll get the supplies we'll need," James says.

"I'll tap into his accounts," Finley adds.

"What will be my role?" Rhett asks.

"You'll sit this one out," I tell him.

"No, he won't," the judge grunts. "He'll prove his worth."

"He's not been trained."

"He's ex-military. I'm sure he can handle himself."

I open my mouth to argue with him, and Rhett's hand is on mine. "He's right. I'll adapt."

"The three of you"—he points to us and James—"will head out tonight. I'll have a small plane ready on the runway."

"What are you going to do?" I cross my arms.

"I'm going to sit this one out. I have bigger fish to fry with the nursing home project. I trust you to handle it without any issues."

"I've typed up all the information you need to know about Fredrick," Finley adds. "It's all in the files, including the fact that he bought the supplies for an underground bunker a few years ago."

"This I'll enjoy," James rubs her hands together.

"Don't leave him with a penny," my father says, getting to his feet, "and don't get caught."

"Go home, get a change of clothes. Make sure it's all black. We'll pick you up when everything is ready."

I kiss Rhett and shove him out the door. The next several hours, I work with Finley, tracking his bank accounts. "We'll need passwords," she says.

"We'll get them."

James hauls two backpacks into the room. "Ready?"

I nod. "He'll never know what hit him."

We take the gear to Finley's SUV and load it in the back. She drives into town parking outside of Rhett's place, and I run up the stairs. He opens the door on the first knock with a small black bag over his shoulder. Shambles leaps into my arms.

"Hey, girl. I've missed you." She purrs.

"Are you trying to steal my cat?" Rhett teases.

"Your cat?" I laugh.

"You gave her to me, and I'm not giving her back."

"Then I guess I'll just have to move into your place."

He takes the cat out of my arms. "See, Shambles, I told you that tactic would work."

"You're my kind of people." I smack a quick kiss to his lips.

He sets her on the floor and locks the door.

"The plane is already waiting on us. It will be well after dark when we arrive."

"The element of surprise," he says.

"Exactly."

We both get in the back seat, and I lay my head on his shoulder. Finley smiles at me in the rearview mirror.

The plane is small, and there's only room for the three of us, plus the pilot. Finley drops us off and we climb the steps, loading our bags in the storage area and greet the pilot.

"You know I can fly one of these things," Rhett says, buckling in his seat.

"Good to know. That skill could be very useful to us."

Once we are in the air, James takes out the files, and we go over every detail.

"How does this work once we get the money from him?" Rhett asks.

"Depending on how much we find, we divvy it up amongst his victims, minus a fee for our services, which goes directly to the judge. It funds the costs of the next project."

"Sometimes the victims are deceased," James adds. "Then there is more money to spread around. We send it to them anonymously if they aren't the client that hired us."

"We don't profit from it," I explain.

"What is it that you need me to do?"

"James is the expert safecracker. I'll work on the client getting the information we'll need to access his accounts. We'll need you as security and to comb through his belongings to see if we missed anything."

When we land, there is a blacked-out Land

Rover waiting on us. Rhett gets behind the wheel and plugs in the GPS location. It leads us up a winding road of a mountain, with the only thing lighting our path are the headlights.

As we make it near the top, Rhett pulls over. "On foot, it's straight through those trees." He points. "I'll recon first to make sure he's in there."

James unzips a bag and tosses him a black ski mask. "We don't want him to see our faces." Then she hands him a radio and a gun.

"I'm not going to kill anyone," his facial expression grows serious.

"It's loaded with blanks, only intended to scare him if we need to."

I take it from her, clip the radio to my hip, and jump out of the vehicle, pulling the mask over my head.

"We'll wait here until you give us the all clear," I tell him.

Chapter 28
♥ RHETT

THE ONLY SOUND I hear is the wind blowing through the tall, thick trees and the crunching beneath my boots. It reminds me of one of my military missions when we were extracting a government official who had been kidnapped.

I flip on the small flashlight James handed me before I shut the door. I have to remind myself, like I did in the military, that we're the good guys by thinking about Nelly and his family. There's no telling what will happen to them if we can't make this right. The thought of them losing their home and being on the streets is horrible. Nelly will lose his way and any opportunity he has for his future.

Making my way up the last incline, I hit a wall of trees surrounding the perimeter of the wood cabin. The place is completely dark, but there is a car parked outside. It's the same license plate number that was in his file. Finley was very detailed in her task.

I unclip the radio from my hip and hold the button. "His car is parked outside the house, and it's completely dark inside."

"We are on our way," Audrey responds.

A good amount of adrenaline is flowing through my veins, picking up the speed of my heart. I wait and listen to hear footsteps coming toward me and flash my light twice.

James pulls her mask over her face. "I'm going to find the bunker." She disappears into the darkness.

"Are you ready?" Audrey blows out a puff of air.

"Yes."

We ease our way onto the steps, and Audrey takes out tools to pick the lock.

"I'm betting he thinks he's safe enough up here he didn't even lock the door." I twist it, and it opens. "He has no outside cameras, and he doesn't think anyone is looking for him."

We tiptoe inside. "Take out your gun," she whispers and slowly opens a door. Fredrick is lying in the middle of a double bed, snoring. Audrey gets her mask in place, and I walk over to the bed. She shines a light in his eyes, and he casually stretches at first, then his eyes pop wide open. I press the tip of the gun to his forehead.

"Don't move," Audrey tells him.

"What do you want?" His voice wavers.

"You've been a naughty boy, stealing other people's life savings, and you're going to repay it tenfold."

"I don't know what you're talking about. You've got the wrong person."

"Lie to me again, and he pulls the trigger." She cocks her head to the side.

I know the gun is carrying blanks, but if I were in his shoes, I'd believe her.

"Get to your feet," she demands, throwing his covers on the floor and leaving him in only boxers.

"I'll do whatever you want. Just don't shoot me." His hands go in the air when his bare feet hit the wood floor.

"You're going to give me the passwords to all of your bank accounts."

He walks out to the living area and sits at a desk, opening a drawer and handing Audrey a small spiral notebook.

She flips through the pages. "This isn't all of them."

"It's all I have. I swear."

"Lie number two." She holds up two fingers.

I play the part well cocking the gun.

"Alright, alright!" he cries and reaches under the desk, taking a sheet of paper from the underside of it.

"Do you have a safe?"

"No."

"Check the house," she tells me, relieving me of the gun. "You log onto your computer."

"Why? I gave you the passwords."

"Just do it," I hear her bite out as I open closets.

"Open each of these accounts," she orders.

I'm sure he's grinding his teeth but complying.

I find a bag at the back of the closet, covered by blankets. Unzipping it, I smile. "Bingo."

Audrey calls my name from the other room, and I lift the bag from the ground, carrying it into the living room, tilting the bag so she can see the stacks of cash.

She hands me the gun. "Keep an eye on him."

I take it, and she nudges Kinsley out of the chair and starts plugging in bank account numbers using one hand.

"Whoever you're working for, I can pay them cash."

"You won't have any money left by the time we're done."

"This is insane." He pulls at his hair with both his hands. "You're bleeding me dry!"

"Just like you did your victims," I growl.

"Who the hell are you?"

"Your worst nightmare," she tells him. "Turn around."

"Keep your hands in the air," I say, and he keeps his back to Audrey.

I watch her skillfully handle the accounts and then change his passwords, each to over sixteen characters.

"That part is done." She stands, and Kinsley leans over the chair, tapping the keys.

"You changed my passwords."

"And your access. It's retinal access only."

"You bitch!"

I shove my shoulder into his chest and my knee at his groin, pinning him against the wall before he can strike Audrey. "You don't want to lay a hand on her," I spat.

"You got what you wanted. Now get out!"

"I'm far from done with you."

James comes barreling through the door and flips on the overhead light. "I emptied the bunker."

"How the hell did you know about my bunker!" His face looks demonic as his lips curl.

"Let's just say we are very good at our jobs. Now for this cabin..."

"I'm not giving you my house."

She takes a lighter from her pocket. "I'm not asking you to give it to me. This place was your grandfather's. He made the mistake of leaving it to you."

"Burn it down. I'll collect the insurance."

Audrey laughs. "It's been canceled."

"What the fuck!"

"Get his keys." She points to a hook by the door.

"Drive it off the side of the mountain."

"You can't leave me with nothing!"

"I can and I will. You didn't give your victims any options. Why should you be any different?" She shrugs.

"I'll go to the police."

"Be my guest. I have a detailed record of all your crimes and the proof to back it up."

"Take him out back and tie him to a tree. Make sure he gets a good view of this place going up in flames. If we're lucky, the wolves will get him."

"No! You can't leave me out here with nothing!" he screams as I shove him out the door.

James throws me a bundle of rope.

"This one will do," I say, backing him against the bark of a tree.

James knots his hands together behind the tree and snaps the rope tight. "He won't be going anywhere until someone frees him," she says. "If you're lucky, they'll see the flames and be here tonight. If not, it could be a couple of days." She walks over and picks up bags, dragging them on the ground, heading in the direction we walked to get here.

A popping sound and orange flames creep up the curtains in the house, and Audrey walks out of the smoke. "We're done now," she tells him, slapping him on the cheek. "If I ever get word of you stealing from another person, I'll be back."

He yells for help as we make our way down the hill. James is already behind the wheel, and we drive back to the airplane in silence. Within minutes, James and Audrey are sound asleep as if nothing out of the ordinary happened tonight.

For them, I guess it didn't. For me, it changed me. I've been a broken man living without purpose, and now I've found it in the oddest of ways. I've never thought of myself as morally gray, but I crossed a line tonight I can't come back from, nor do I want to. Nelly's family will be okay, and I can live with that. It's attracted me to Audrey even more, if that's possible. Her professional looks and demeanor are deceiving. She hides her soft spots and sympathetic heart well. She's fierce and vulnerable at the same time. I love her heart and how she feels in my arms. There isn't anything I wouldn't do for this woman.

Chapter 29
♥ AUDREY

FINLEY PICKS us up in the wee hours of the morning, and I'm exhausted by the time she pulls up in front of Rhett's apartment. He looks surprised when I follow him up the stairs and wave at Finley as she drives off.

"You're staying with me?" he asks, unlocking the door.

"Unless you'd rather I not." I lift a single brow.

He hangs the key on a hook and shuffles out of his shoes. "There's no place I'd rather you be."

"Good." I smile and take his hand, leading him to the bedroom.

We both silently strip out of our clothes and crawl into bed. "Your hair smells like burning embers," he nuzzles my neck, pressing his chest to my back.

"You can wash it for me after about eight hours of sleep."

He exhales and is asleep within minutes.

My heart is full. He didn't shy away after the

things he saw and heard tonight. I clutch my charm. "He truly is the man for me, Momma," I whisper.

I'm not going to let the judge pull us apart again. After last night, he's proven how much he wants to be a part of my life. I know it won't be easy, but he'll have to find a way to accept him, and perhaps one day, they can even be golfing buddies again.

Shambles jumps up on the bed and curls between us like a child would do. For the first time, the possibility of having a child of my own could be a reality. I shake my head. Not for me. Our lives are too dangerous. I leave the children for James. She's free now to be happy.

With that thought, I drift off to sleep in the arms of the man I love.

* * *

I stretch and see the time. It's five in the afternoon, and the sheets next to me are cool. "Rhett," I call his name. The apartment is quiet except for Shambles, who is meowing.

"Where is he, girl?" I get up and go to the bathroom, then wash my face. I walk out of the bedroom and see a note lying on the counter.

• • •

Your father called and wanted to meet with me. You were sleeping so soundly I didn't want to wake you.

"Shit!" I fumble to put my shoes on and run down the steps, only to remember I didn't drive. Peering down the road, I see the judge's car parked down the block in front of the Bond & Bevel.

I waste no time crossing the street, nearly getting taken out by a car.

"Use the crosswalk, lady!" the driver screams.

I rush inside when a customer opens the door to the coffee shop, and I see Rhett's door is closed. It's never closed.

Thomas sees me and smiles.

"Is he in his office?"

"Yeah, he's been locked in there for about an hour with some old dude."

I press my lips together and don't bother knocking, bursting inside. I'm surprised when I see the two of them laughing.

"What are you doing here?"

Rhett gets to his feet and walks over to me, shutting the door and wrapping his arms around my waist. "It's okay. Everything is going to be alright."

"James told me what all went down. If Rhett is

going to be part of this family, I needed to make amends with him. I could still use a golfing partner."

"You scared me to death with your note. I thought he was going to kill you." I lay my hand on his chest.

"You don't have to worry about that anymore. He's given us his blessing to be together."

He sits, and I sit in his lap. "Thank you."

"There's enough money to take care of the Nelsons' hospital bill and replace his savings along with paying off the second mortgage on their home."

"That's great news."

"Nine other families will also receive monies that he stole from them."

"I can't wait to tell Nelly's mom."

The judge leans his elbows on the desk. "Here's the thing. They didn't hire us, so you can't tell them anything."

"Oh, right."

"The money will just show up in their bank account, thanks to my other talented daughter, Finley."

"Then I can't wait to hear the excitement in her voice when she tells me their bills are paid." Rhett smacks a kiss to my lips.

He stands. "Don't forget we have another job lined up. I'll see you on the golf course Friday."

Rhett scoots me off his lap. "Noon sharp," he tells him.

My father smooths down his suit jacket and exits the office, leaving the door open.

"That went way better than I expected." I sigh in relief.

"Yeah, me too. I need to go check on Nelly. Do you want to come with me to the hospital?"

"Yes. I'd love to see him. While I'm there, maybe James can change this cast for something a little less cumbersome."

We walk hand in hand down the street. This is what normal couples must feel like, and I'm loving it. Loving him.

We're buzzed into the ICU, and Nelly comes running over and hugs me as soon as he sees me. "What happened to your arm?"

"Nothing serious. I hear your dad is going to be okay."

"Mom says he has a long way to go, but he'll be fine."

"I'm so happy for you."

Mary strolls toward us. "I woke up this morning to all the money that was taken back in my bank account and then some. Did you have anything to do with that?"

"No. I wish I could work magic like that." His hand tightens around mine.

"I wish I could thank whoever got it all back."

"Sometimes, we don't ever get to meet our guardian angels." I grin and lean into Rhett.

"When's our next hockey practice, Coach?" Nelly peers up at Rhett.

"I think it would be alright if you skipped it."

"No way. I want to be there."

"It's fine." His mom ruffles his hair.

"Tomorrow at six."

"I'll be there." He runs back to his dad's room.

"Thank you so much for all the support you've given us and for truly caring about my son."

"He's a good kid."

She smiles and returns to her husband's side.

"I want to stop in the ER and see James."

"Sure. While you're talking to her, I need to make a few phone calls."

We ride the elevator to the first floor, and the lady at the front desk points to where I can find James.

"Hey," she says when she sees me. "What are you doing here?"

I hold my cast out in front of me. "Can you take this thing off?"

"No. It's not healed yet."

"How about a lighter one?"

"That's the one the orthopedic surgeon wants you to wear until your next appointment."

"It's a pain in the ass."

"Just like its owner." She balks at my request. "Please tell me you're still moving out."

"I've postponed it for a while. The judge and I had a long, meaningful conversation, and I think he's willing to lighten up a bit."

"Really?" I question.

"Time will tell. You two look good together." She angles her head toward Rhett, who is leaning against a wall with his phone pressed to his ear.

"We do, don't we." I feel my insides warm up just admiring him.

"He's perfect for you. It gives me lots of hope for myself."

"You'll find someone. You're too good of a person not to." I hug her one-armed and then lead Rhett out of the hospital.

He ends his conversation and cuddles me to his side. "Where are we headed now?"

"Back to your place. Someone promised to wash my hair."

"Does that include the rest of your body?" His eyes darken.

"Every inch of me," I beam.

"This author has the magical ability to take an already strong and interesting plot and add so many unexpected twists and turns that it turns her books into a complete addiction for the reader." Dandelion Inspired Blog

Signup for all the latest news and receive a free book:

Newsletter

Armed with books in the crook of my elbow, I can go anywhere. That's my philosophy! Better yet, I'll write the books that will take me on an adventure.

My heroes are a bit broken but will make you swoon. My heroines are their own kick-ass characters armed with humor and a plethora of sarcasm.

If I'm not tucked away in my writing den, with coffee firmly gripped in hand, you can find me with a book propped on my pillow, a pit bull lying across my legs, a Lab on the floor next to me, and two kittens running amuck.

My current adventure has me living in Idaho with my own gray-bearded hero, who's put up with my shenanigans for over thirty years, and he doesn't mind all my book boyfriends.

If you love romance, suspense, military men, lots of action and adventure infused with emotion, tear-worthy moments, and laugh-out-loud humor, dive into my books and let the world fall away at your feet.

series by kelly moore

Whiskey River West

Whiskey River Road

Elite Six Series

The Revenge You Seek

The Vigilante Hitman

August Series

Epic Love Stories

For more follow me on Amazon for a detailed list of books.

Or, on my website at kellymooreauthor.com